Rogue

The Honorable Rogues®, Book Six

COLLETTE CAMERON

Blue Rose Romance®
Portland, Oregon

Sweet-to-Spicy Timeless Romance®

A ROSE FOR A ROGUE
The Honorable Rogues®, Book Six
Copyright © 2018 Collette Cameron
Cover Design by: Darlene Albert

This book is a work of fiction. Names, characters, places, and incidents are the product of the author's imagination or are used fictitiously. Any resemblance to actual events, locales, or persons, living or dead, is coincidental.

All rights reserved under International and Pan-American Copyright Conventions. By downloading or purchasing a print copy of this book, you have been granted the non-exclusive, non-transferable right to access and read the text of this book. No part of this text may be reproduced, transmitted, downloaded, decompiled, reverse engineered, or stored in or introduced into any information storage and retrieval system, in any form or by any means, whether electronic or mechanical, now known or hereinafter invented without the express written permission of copyright owner.

Attn: Permissions Coordinator
Blue Rose Romance®
8420 N Ivanhoe # 83054
Portland, Oregon 97203

eBook ISBN: 9781954307490
Paperback ISBN: 9781954307506

www.collettecameron.com

"Mistress?"

His voice went deep and velvety.

Wholly mesmerizing. Wonderfully wicked.

"An interesting notion."

"A deeply heartfelt, beautifully written story about two mismatched lovers who are perfect for each other. Truly charming."
~*Vanessa Kelly USA Today Bestselling Author*

Other Collette Cameron Books

The Honorable Rogues®
A Kiss for a Rogue
A Bride for a Rogue
A Rogue's Scandalous Wish
To Capture a Rogue's Heart
The Rogue and the Wallflower
A Rose for a Rogue

Check out Collette's Other Series
Castle Brides
Highland Heather Romancing a Scot
Daughters of Desire (Scandalous Ladies)
The Blue Rose Regency Romances:
The Culpepper Misses
Seductive Scoundrels
Heart of a Scot

Collections
Lords in Love
The Honorable Rogues® Books 1-3
The Honorable Rogues® Books 4-6
Seductive Scoundrels Series Books 1-3
Seductive Scoundrels Series Books 4-6
The Blue Rose Regency Romances-
The Culpepper Misses Series 1-2

Dedication

To all the Mr. Wiggles and their owners everywhere.

May you experience the unconditional

love only a dog can give you.

(Okay, cats can too!)

Acknowledgements

A huge thanks to my VIP Reader Group, Collette's Chèris, for helping pick Chester's middle names, and to Amy Ikari for suggesting Acorn for Eden's pet squirrel's name. The pet squirrel was inspired by my sister Holly's pine squirrel, Orbit. Thank you to Darlene Albert for A ROSE FOR A ROGUE's gorgeous cover, Period Images for the models who posed for the exclusive shoot, Kathryn Lynn Davis and Emilee Bowers for your fabulous editing, and as always, my assistants, Cindy Jackson and Dee Foster.

1

Newbury, Berkshire England
27 May 1820

Dilly dallying and dawdling weren't going to change anything.

Manchester, Marquis of Sterling, tossed back the last of the fairly decent whisky. With a resigned sigh, he placed his empty glass on the Fox and Falcon's time-worn countertop. A full bottle wouldn't have succeeded in easing a jot of his tension. Nothing could be done for the darkling thoughts tumbling round inside his skull either.

What few feeble rays of late afternoon sunlight managed to escape the sodden clouds outside filtered through the lace curtains bordering the pristine windowpanes. He permitted a small, wry smile to tip his mouth. From what he'd observed since leading Magnus into Newbury almost two hours ago, except for the shutters' new coat of bright cobalt paint, the pub—along with the picturesque township—had changed little in his ten-year absence.

Had it truly been a decade since he'd strolled Newbury's streets, attended the century-old, two-story stone church Sunday mornings, sneaked his first and last cheroot behind the stables, shared a dram with friends in this very establishment, or returned the friendly villagers' many greetings?

A third of his life.

Now that the old duke's health was failing, he'd been summoned—*ordered*—home.

No. Not home.

Perygrim Park had ceased being home the day his sire blamed Chester for Byron's death, whilst also beckoning every curse from hell upon the Andrews of Gablecrest Hall.

His father's venomous words, shrieked

hysterically as he cradled his favorite son in his arms, still echoed in Chester's memory—still lanced his heart even after all these years.

He cut a longing glance toward the whisky bottle.

Did he dare?

Even to silence the silent monologue ever ready to torment him?

Russell Stewart, the pub's owner, angled his jowly chin toward the deep green half-full bottle whilst drying a glass.

"Would you care for another tot, my lord? Or perhaps some of my missus's shepherd's pie?"

If only he might. The fading light confirmed the sun's slow descent, and he'd promised to arrive at Perygrim in time for dinner.

To celebrate his thirtieth birthday.

Many were the ways he'd have preferred to acknowledge the date, none of which included being scowled at and mocked by a spiteful curmudgeon. A cantankerous sod whose infrequent letters oozed with criticism, condemnation, complaints about Chester's failure to marry and produce an heir, and fiendish gloating when Walter Andrews had drowned several years ago in the lake betwixt Perygrim Park's and Gablecrest Hall's lands.

Curse Chester's sense of duty. His endless guilt.

A pox on the miniscule tender spot for his father remaining inside the buttress he'd erected around his battered heart.

He drew in a steadying breath, then released it in a long, controlled exhale.

The old man was dying.

Despite his sire's rancor, Chester couldn't be so cruel as to deny his critically ill father's one last request. Honestly, this visit was more about putting to rest the phantoms haunting Chester once and for all than about reconciling with the duke.

He filled his lungs with another fortifying breath and closed his eyes for an instant when his stomach released a discontented growl.

"You were always particularly fond of Jane's roast beef and potatoes too, sir. Are you sure you won't have a plate?"

Stewart wiped the already immaculate counter, his

hint as obvious as the single bushy eyebrow spanning his broad forehead.

Whisky on an empty stomach never boded well. Particularly since Chester generally eschewed spirits stronger than wine.

Unlike the sixth Duke of DeCourcy.

Diligence and discipline.

That mantra, Chester's life's motto, set him apart from his embittered sire.

"No, thank you, though I well remember Mrs. Stewart's pie." Shaking his head, Chester fished in his pocket for a few coins. "Another time, I give you my word. I quite look forward to it."

After laying the money on the smooth walnut—battling the urge to slap them down and vent some of his pent-up frustration—he collected his beaver hat.

He'd have made Perygrim some time ago if Magnus hadn't picked up a stone a quarter mile back and required tending. The horse's misfortune provided him a much-needed respite before facing the dragon who'd begat him.

Holding his tongue might prove Chester's greatest

trial.

Diligence and discipline, man. You were not cast from the same malformed mold.

He barely contained a derisive snort.

But I am a product of his loins.

Stewart collected the coins, smiling broadly and revealing the rabbit-like front teeth Chester remembered so well.

"I know I speak for others as well as myself when I say we're pleased you've returned, m'lord. I'll make sure to stock that Bordeaux you're fond of in the future, and I'll bet my missus will keep a fresh supply of Sally Lund buns on hand now too."

"Thank you. All the more reason to return very soon."

Chester scanned the cozy taproom again. How many times had he and Byron enjoyed a dark ale whilst bantering with and razzing each other, as brothers are wont to do?

One elbow resting on the bar, he inclined his head.

"I've missed this, Stewart. Missed Newbury and her citizens."

Truly, he had.

He far preferred the country's serene pace than teeming Town life, which was why he attended nearly every country house party he'd been invited to these past years.

"I hope you'll honor us with your presence often, m'lord." Touching his fingers to his brow, Stewart angled his stout form toward the kitchen. "I'll have your mount brought 'round now."

With another nod, Chester pulled on a black leather glove as he marched to the entrance, acknowledging the curious, slightly leery patrons observing his progress with a smile or a nod. They'd find him much more approachable, friendlier, and fairer than the current duke. He'd make sure of that.

No more whispers about DeCourcy the Demon Duke. Devilish and dastardly duke too.

Maybe he'd strive for a new moniker, something a trifle more flattering to the duchy.

The Dancing Duke?

No, too frivolous.

Perchance the Dashing Duke?

Pompous and full of self-importance.

The Dignified Duke?

A memory sparked—swimming nude in the lake, something he intended to do again now that he had returned home. Nothing remotely dignified about that.

He reached to press the latch when the door sprang open, practically smacking him in the face. The sturdy panel came to an abrupt halt when the wood hit his boots. His injured toes curled in protest despite their stout leather protection.

Arms laden, a petite, dull brown-clad flurry barreled into him, whacked her forehead on his chest and, giving a startled squeal, dropped one of her baskets.

Eggs and greens scattered everywhere, including atop his feet, and he instinctively clutched her elbows to keep her from crashing to the scuffed floor too.

A whiff of roses and lilies and some other essence wafted upward. Nostrils flared, he inhaled, trying to decipher the other scents. Perhaps a tinge of orange blossom or lemon? Fresh and light and wholly memorable.

"I beg your pardon."

Breathless, the top of her head not quite at shoulder level, she arched away, peering upward.

Her hood slipped off to reveal unbound hair, a shade somewhere between walnut and pecan. Not brown exactly, but not blonde either, though golden ribbons threaded the strands here and there.

Her pale, ice blue eyes—*hyacinth blue*—rounded in surprise but not embarrassment. A deeper azure green rimmed her irises which, if he wasn't mistaken, shimmered with uncontained joy and ill-concealed amusement.

Directed at him.

Battling an inexplicable reluctance to do so, he set her from him. Not, however, before mentally noting the delicacy of the arms his fingers encircled or the refined planes of her flushed face. Or her bowed mouth, pinkish-red from the brisker-than-usual May air.

Since when did he notice a woman's hair color?

Or wind-tinted lips, for that matter?

Must be the whisky—had him numpty. Which was

why he rarely imbibed more than a single tot.

Disgruntled at his intense, unsolicited, and distracting reaction, he firmed his mouth whilst leveling her a reproving glance.

"Perhaps you ought to watch where you're going and use more caution when opening doors."

"Indeed, I should, sir."

Not the least chagrined, she offered a winsome smile, and the most irregular sensation flickered in his chest.

Bloody whisky.

How could something so simple, the upward turn of her petal soft lips, transform her heretofore unremarkable features into breathtaking beauty?

And more on point, why ever had he noticed?

Because a man could fall in love with that radiant smile.

He shook his head.

By Jove, he hadn't indulged enough to produce *those* kinds of fanciful musings.

Not he, the master of controlling his baser instincts and dark inclinations.

"Russell, might I have a towel or two?" the small tempest called to the innkeeper as she crouched and gave a rueful twist of her pretty rose bud mouth at the mess she'd made. After placing the other basket on the floor, she gathered the salvageable herbs.

The odors of crushed oregano, rosemary, sage, and other aromatic plants Chester couldn't identify drifted upward.

Who was she?

Obviously, someone who'd moved here after Father disowned him. Though her simple cloak and the scuffed half-boots peeking from the practical woolen folds of her russet colored gown weren't the first stare of fashion, neither were they the coarse garments of a commoner.

A young, lonely widow perhaps?

From beneath half-closed eyes, he scrutinized her, very much liking what he saw.

Not attractive in the classical sense, nonetheless, an unidentifiable allure surrounded her. Beckoned him. Caused unruly thoughts and inclinations to knock about ribs.

Most troubling were these rash musings. They bespoke a ruthlessness, an inherited characteristic always—*always until now*—meticulously controlled, lest he mirror the duke's scurrilous behavior or tendencies.

Brushing his bare hand over his mouth and jaw, Chester narrowed his eyes.

He'd never entertained the notion of a mistress before, particularly upon just meeting a woman. But he'd need something—someone—to keep him sane the next few weeks or months.

She might prove just the tantalizing distraction he needed.

Stewart poked his oversized head around the doorframe leading to the kitchen. "Missus, Miss Eden's had a mishap. She needs help cleaning it up."

Miss Eden?

Not a widow then. Bother that. Chester didn't dally with innocents, no matter how bewitching their smiles or innocently seductive their eyes might be.

Unwarranted disappointment constricted his ribs.

"What's this?" Bearing damp cloths, Mrs. Stewart

bustled from the kitchen, her round cheeks apple-red from toiling over the hot stove, no doubt. Upon spying the slimy mess, she *tsked* and *tutted*. "Miss Eden, I'd about given up on you coming today."

A shadow dimmed Miss Eden's bubbly countenance as she accepted the linens. But only for an instant before her cheery smile returned full on.

"Alas, Mama had a difficult morning, and I wasn't able to leave as early as I'd planned. But I promised I'd deliver eggs and herbs today, so here I am." A rueful smile teased the corners of her mouth. "Those plants are a little battered, I'm afraid."

Pointing at the basket holding the crushed greens, she curved her full mouth upward again, and Chester forced his attention away from her glowing face.

And those tempting bowed lips.

Women smiled at him all the time.

Incredibly beautiful and perfumed women. Many who regularly offered him much more than a radiant upward tilting of their rouged mouths. Elegant, coiffed, and graceful ladies, keen and qualified to be the next Duchess of DeCourcy. All the more puzzling then, why this little nondescript country mouse had him gawking like a young, untried buck.

"I don't know what I'd do without your conservatory, Miss Eden."

Mrs. Stewart lifted a bay sprig and held it to her nose. "I'd like lavender next time too, if you have any. I've a mind to try a lavender shortbread recipe my sister sent me."

"I do, and mint as well. I know you enjoy mint tea."

The young woman fluttered her ungloved fingers at the other basket. Short oval nails graced her small, elegant hands, which weren't as milky white or soft as the ladies of his acquaintance.

"I've brought jars of honey to sell, and a present for you, Jane. Give me a minute to clean up the mess I've made."

Thank God she hadn't also dropped the honey. Eggs were bad enough, but honey was a sticky horror.

Without hesitation, she proceeded to wipe egg yolk and parsley off Chester's less than gleaming boots. Trekking the last quarter mile along the mucky lane had caked his Wellingtons with a thick layer of mud. Though he'd scraped his feet before entering the Fox and Falcon, considerable filth remained.

"Here now, miss. There's no need for that."

He backed up a pair of paces. It unsettled him to have this pretty little thing kneeling, mopping at his splattered boots like the meanest of servants.

"Are you certain? A distinguished gentleman such as yourself cannot very well toddle off with yolk and shell sticking to your boots."

Sarcasm?

Marquises didn't toddle.

Well, perhaps if they'd unwisely drunk more than they ought on an empty stomach and were a trifle foxed, they might.

"Can you imagine what the villagers might say?"

She lifted a large piece of dark speckled eggshell from his toe.

Was she mocking him?

Lowering his lashes halfway, he considered her.

She pushed her hair behind her ear, and a troubled frown furrowed her brow, drawing his attention to the pea-sized birthmark near her hairline on the right side.

"Oh, you're probably worried about me ruining the boot leather." She scratched her eyebrow, unease now crimping the edges of her expressive eyes. "I'm certain there must be someone in town who can care for them. Maybe not at this hour, though."

Mouth pursed, she picked another bit of shell from the leather.

He pulled on his other glove and gave her a reassuring smile.

"You misunderstand me. There's no need to fuss over them. I'll clean and polish my boots this evening."

A little furrow of surprise marred her forehead. "You will? Polish them yourself? But you're a gentleman. I didn't think . . ."

She sounded so incredulous, he wasn't sure whether to be enchanted or insulted.

"I am, but I'm not above tending to my own boots." He sketched a bow, more elaborate than the situation called for. "Manchester, Marquis of Sterling. And you are Miss Eden."

She narrowed her eyes and raked her astute regard over him, from his beaver hat, down the length of his great coat to his soiled boots, and then made the reverse journey to meet his eyes once more.

His flesh reacted—the nerves and pores alert and expectant—with every slow inch of her perusal.

Did her thorough assessment mean she knew who he was?

It was hardly a secret.

She had him at a disadvantage then, for he hadn't an inkling who Miss Eden might be.

"Not Miss Eden exactly," she finally said, the amused sparkle returning to her eyes.

"No?"

She shook her head and that cloud of downy hair billowed around her shoulders.

Unusual to leave her hair down. Not the fashion at all, but he quite admired the shiny mass.

She chuckled, a lyrical warble, causing a weird flitting about in his chest again.

He really must leave off strong spirits if this was how they'd begun to affect him.

Or perchance the expectation of seeing his sire after a decade was causing his heart palpitations.

As she straightened, she passed Jane the soiled toweling.

"Eden is my middle name."

She bobbed a curtsy that would've earned even Almack's stern peeresses' approval.

"Eglantina Eden Aster Haverden."

Eglantina?

Chester couldn't prevent his gaze from falling on the unbroken eggs.

Egg?

Zounds, why would anyone name a child that? He could well imagine the teasing her name had inspired.

A delightful laugh escaped her as she caught his reaction.

"I know, it's uncommon. Mama says it means wild rose. I prefer my first middle name, Eden." She dipped into a shallow curtsy. "I beg your pardon again, my lord."

After another brilliant smile that left him blinking like a codpated buffoon, she picked up her baskets and whisked into the kitchen behind Mrs. Stewart.

A grin playing around the edges of his mouth, Chester cut a wave toward Stewart and then made his way outside. Remarkable how that small bundle of feminine energy had lifted his spirits like nothing else had in a great while.

Reins in hand, a young ostler waited with Magnus beside a much-used dogcart pulled by a pretty bay mare—wearing a hideous straw hat, complete with purple and orange silk flowers.

Upon the wagon's seat sat the most pathetic excuse for a canine Chester had ever seen. Of an undistinguishable breed, one raggedy black ear stood straight up and the other ear—this one grayish-beige—drooped onto its forehead. Its brandy-colored gaze remained fixed on the doorway Chester had just exited. And the whole while, its tongue peeking from the side of its mouth, the dog appeared to grin. A bright yellow ribbon tied in a large floppy bow graced the mutt's mottled neck.

Still ugly as sin, and a waste of good ribbon.

Chester angled his head toward the creature,

which spared him the briefest glance before training his avid attention on the pub once more.

"Eden Haverden's?"

An ear-to-ear grin split the groom's face, and he nodded.

"Yes, m'lord. His name is Mr. Wiggles. Miss Eden found him dumped outside Newbury—oh, I guess it'd be about three years ago now."

Wiggles?

Her dog's name was almost as charmingly awful as hers. And God help him, who put a hat—a hideously ugly hat—on their horse?

Eglantina Eden Aster Haverden, that was who.

Who was she?

He knew her name of course, but what had brought her to Newbury? When had she come? What was her story, for everyone had a tale? Often more than one. Some they'd rather keep secret.

Why, devil take it, was he so interested?

He surveyed the street as he accepted Magnus's ribbons.

"Your lordship?" With a jerk of his shaggy head,

the ostler indicated the horse's sore foot. "I removed the rock and packed mud, but he has a nasty hoof bruise. You can ride him if you must, but I'd advise stabling him in Newbury for a few days until he heals. Another mount can be had yonder." He pointed down the street. "Or mayhap, Miss Eden can give you a ride. She lives close to Perygrim Park."

He wouldn't risk laming Magnus. The horse meant too much to him, and at thirteen, with proper care, had many good riding years left.

His mount's injury provided Chester a legitimate excuse for delaying his arrival at Perygrim, but at this juncture, he just wanted to have done with the confrontation. Delaying another day or two was cowardly, and he'd never again give the duke an excuse to call him a poltroon.

"Very well. See that he has the best care." He passed the groom a crown as he handed the reins back. "There's double that for you when I return for him."

"Thank you, m'lord. I'll treat him like the prince he is."

With another wide grin, the chap eagerly pocketed

the coin.

Chester let Mr. Wiggles sniff the back of his hand, then scratched the dog's scruffy neck.

Miss Haverden swept out the door, calling lively farewells to those inside.

"I'll be back at the end of the week. The hens are laying better now that it's lighter longer, and the hothouse asparagus is nearly ready."

Pulling up her hood, she glanced at the sulky sky before approaching her wagon.

"I fear we're in for more rain, Benjamin. Peony won't like that at all, even with her hat."

The horse wore a hat because she didn't like the rain?

"For certain, Miss."

Chester hadn't missed the flush tinting Benjamin's freckled face or the swiftly concealed look of adoration he gave her.

Unfamiliar chagrin jolted down Chester's spine. Not only hadn't it occurred to him to ask the groom his name, but something prickly and unpleasant and very much like jealousy needled him.

A first, and he didn't like the sensation.

Her guileless attention swung to her dog.

"Ah, I see you've met Mr. Wiggles. He's quite a love."

Whining, the animal stood as she approached, shaking his scraggly tail furiously.

In that instant, Chester made a decision and dispensed with etiquette.

Discipline and vigilance, his conscience upbraided. *Vigilance and discipline.*

Bugger off, he silently retorted.

Nothing and no one had intrigued him or piqued his interest as much as this imp in a goodly while.

"If it wouldn't be a terrible inconvenience, may I prevail upon you for a ride?" He flashed her a smile designed to liquefy steel. He didn't normally bother with such calculated drivel, but something about the enigmatic Miss Eden was causing him to cast off his usual reticence.

Her soft, kissable mouth slackened in surprise at his brazen request.

"My horse has injured his foot, and I fear bearing

my weight will lame him. Benjamin said you live near Perygrim Park."

"For certain you wouldn't want to injure him further."

She approached the horse, and cooing softly, let him catch her scent.

Which, Chester recalled, smelled wonderfully of roses and lilies. Lucky beast.

She ran her petite palm down his neck.

"I'm going to take your master home, but he'll be back to get you in a day or two. All right? I'll send an apple with him for you. Would you like that?"

It mattered naught whether Magnus adored or despised the fruit, for now Chester had an excuse to see this enchanting creature again.

Peony tilted her ears back and whickered.

As she angled toward the cart, Miss Haverden chuckled, and an answering bubbling rose in his chest at the musical, mirth-filled sound.

"No need to be jealous, Peony. You can have an apple, too. As if I don't give you one every day."

Before he could offer his assistance, she dropped

her baskets in the wagon bed and deftly climbed into the seat, revealing a trim calf in the process. At once, Mr. Wiggles clambered to her side, and she kissed his forehead whilst scratching his scruffy ears.

She cocked her head and indicated the remaining bench.

"My lord, if you please. The sun is setting, and with the mucky road, it will take at least five and forty minutes to reach Perygrim Park."

"You know the way?"

He settled himself on the seat, feeling oddly chastised, and Mr. Wiggles thumped his tail once in a cautious greeting.

"I do, though I've never actually been as far as the manor house itself."

Clucking her tongue, she shook the ribbons once.

"Walk on, Peony."

The horse swished her ebony tail, then with a groan and creak, the cart lurched forward. For a few minutes, only the clattering of the wheels and the clopping of Peony's hooves broke the companionable silence.

Staring straight ahead, Miss Haverden skillfully

maneuvered the wagon along the busy street. Every now and again, a villager raised their hand, and she waved in return. Many more stopped and stared as the dogcart rattled past, their avid curiosity evident.

"I'm afraid I can only take you as far as the outer drive." She cut him a swift sideways glance before returning her attention to the cobbled road. "I'm forbidden to go farther."

Forbidden?

That was an interesting turn of phrase.

He angled toward her to better see her expression. Running a hand down Mr. Wiggle's spine—for which he was rewarded with a doggy grin—he regarded her.

"Forbidden? Why?"

A small smile quirked her lush mouth.

"His Grace has banned all Andrews from his property."

"But you aren't an Andrews." Premonition had Chester tightening his buttocks on the inhospitable seat. "Are you?"

She turned that clear azure-eyed gaze upon him and peered straight into his soul.

"I'm Walter Andrews's illegitimate daughter."

2

Eden swallowed a giggle at the utterly flummoxed expression on the sharply hewn angles of Lord Sterling's beautifully sculpted face.

Even Mr. Wiggles cocked his head and twitched his ears.

Perhaps she ought to have couched that tidbit about her bastardry with a warning. But she'd wanted to test Lord Sterling's response. She'd better hope he remained the gentleman, too, since she'd unwisely agreed to take him, an utter stranger, to Perygrim, and they'd no chaperone.

Bosh. What balderdash. Three and twenty-year-old spinsters didn't require chaperones.

Lord Sterling stared at her, those eyes, gray one minute and green the next, his firm lips pressed together just the merest bit, further testament to his consternation.

She'd really flabbergasted him, poor man.

Her stomach flip-flopped peculiarly. Just like it had in the pub when his lordship had turned those gray-green, black-lashed eyes on her with such intensity. She was hard pressed not to squirm on the seat. At least she was prepared for her response to him now.

Then why did dragonfly wings flutter in her pulse, even as his masculinity snared her reluctant attention?

Really, it was most unfair that he should have such beautiful eyes. Soft and gray, like a baby bunny's silky fur one minute, and jeweled green the next. How was a woman, especially a country sparrow unaccustomed to lords, supposed to resist their intoxicating draw?

That awkward moment when she'd plowed into him in the Fox and Falcon, he'd so disconcerted her, she'd dropped her egg basket. Or maybe it had been the disturbingly wide spans of his solid chest beneath her cheek that knocked her breath from her momentarily and caused her to lose her grip on the handle.

A pleasant, clean, masculine smell with a hint of horse and leather surrounded him. She'd battled the oddest urge to nestle closer and sniff.

He'd blamed her clumsiness on haste.

She far preferred that misconception to his knowing the immediate and overwhelming attraction engulfing her. That instant magnetism, the awareness of him as a virile man in a way no other man had ever affected her, utterly terrified her.

Hot, intoxicating temptation radiated from him.

Until now, she'd never understood nor experienced sexual desire, but what other explanation could there be for these errant flickers or the heat sidling about in her veins?

Resolution thrummed through her, and she pulled her spine straight whilst erecting a barrier of self-protection.

She would not end up like Mama.

Well, of course she wouldn't.

First and foremost, Mama had never found Walter Andrews the least appealing, and secondly, to all intents and purposes, Lord Sterling was the enemy.

Not Eden's enemy exactly; she scarce knew the man.

But any relation of the Duke of DeCourcy was an avowed adversary of the Andrews. The reverse was true as well.

Only she wasn't an Andrews.

Not legally, in any event.

How Simon Andrews would gnash his teeth if he learned she had even spoken to the marquis, let alone given him a ride. Well, what her half-brother didn't know couldn't hurt. Besides, not only was she past her majority, it was far past time this stupid feud between the Andrews and the DeCourcys ended.

She wasn't sure she knew how it had begun a decade ago, but she had heard whispers and rumors. Mostly from the townspeople. Something to do with Simon and the duke's eldest son claiming to have downed the same trophy stag.

Sheer ridiculousness if that was truly the cause of

the rift. To declare an affair of honor over a red deer's antlers. Certainly not worth a man dying for, or families—once the closest of friends—becoming sworn enemies.

Tattle also claimed Lord Sterling and the duke were estranged.

His Grace's failing health was no secret, and for days the village had been atwitter in anticipation of the marquis's imminent return.

"I wasn't aware Andrews had another daughter."

Clearing his throat, his lordship repositioned his hat atop his wavy auburn hair, a rich dark mahogany. Quite the most unusual shade she'd ever seen.

She lifted a shoulder whilst steering Peony through the neat mossy stone pillars on the village outskirts.

"It's a poorly kept secret, of which I'm certain everyone is aware. Mama and I have lived at Briar Knoll Cottage for a number of years. I was away at school for seven of those. I've been back for eight now. Mama summoned me home when Walter Andrews died."

"I heard of his passing. My condolences."

"Thank you, but they are wasted on me. I never considered him my father."

She would not call that fiend Father. Not even in death.

He'd never been anything more than the man who ruined Mama, despite his regular visits to the cottage, the occasional gifts, and his footing the bill for her boarding school.

Familiar disquiet washed over her, but repeated practice at controlling her expression and temperament around her mother to prevent distressing her, enabled Eden to mask her outrage and resentment.

Everyone believed she possessed an amiable disposition. Fortunate no one could see her gnarled, ugly thoughts. Still, it was one thing to entertain uncharitable musings and another entirely to act upon them.

"I was away at university as well," Lord Sterling remarked in that dark honey baritone, while canting his head contemplatively.

Lord, those eyes.

She looked away, lest he catch her ogling.

"You must concede, it's a rather unusual arrangement. You living on the same property as his heir."

Keeping a forced mistress—the former governess to Walter Andrews's daughters—and a child born on the wrong side of the blanket in a cottage just ten minutes' walk from the manor?

His lordship didn't know the half of it.

If ever a man was dicked in the knob, it had been Walter Andrews. Even his other daughters, Florence and Harriette, the ones Mama had been governess too, had rarely visited when their sire was alive and did so even less frequently since his death.

Giving Lord Sterling a considering look, Eden detected none of the typical censure or judgment the upper class generally bestowed upon her. Interest more than anything glinted in his compelling gaze.

"It is unusual, I concede."

"It is."

They jostled along in silence again for several minutes. After his extended absence, likely his lordship had much on his mind. Niggling worry about Mama's fainting this morning continued to plague Eden.

She doubted they'd make Perygrim before rainfall began again. A swift perusal of the grumpy heavens confirmed her suspicion.

"Miss Haverden?"

She glanced at Lord Sterling, sitting but inches from her.

He wasn't looking at her, but instead gazed at the road before them.

Mr. Wiggle's torso and snout lay across his lordship's lap.

"My mother is Miss Haverden. I'm simply Miss Eden."

He acknowledged this with a slight nod.

"I would hope that the quarrel between my father and your brother doesn't prohibit us from furthering our acquaintance."

The apologetic smile he sent Eden reminded her of Simon's sons: eight-year-old Timothy and six-year-old Prentice. Such sweetly disposed boys, and polite. A true wonder, given their haughty and difficult parents.

Every chance they could, her nephews sneaked to Briar Knoll for hot chocolate, Mattie's Shrewsbury biscuits, and to play with Mr. Wiggles and Eden's pet squirrel, Acorn.

When next they came, there'd be newly hatched chicks too.

Mayhap, she'd let them each choose one for a pet, since neither Simon nor his wife Candace permitted the boys that rite of passage.

As they approached the small-planked bridge spanning Black Beck's swollen banks, she adjusted her rump, braced her feet, and slowed Peony.

"My lord, the squabble aside, why would you want to further our association? You're the next Duke of DeCourcy. I'm the by-blow of landed gentry. The daughter of a governess. And in case you hadn't noticed," she waffled her hand at Peony, Mr. Wiggles, and finally her streaming hair, "I'm a bit unconventional. Such association would only incite gossip, something I'd rather avoid. I'm certain you can appreciate why."

"May I speak plainly?"

The breeze teased the slightly curly hair skimming his collar.

"I'd prefer that you do. I cannot abide hedging."

She nodded, and her hood slid off. They'd made the old stone-sided bridge, so she didn't dare take a hand off the reins. Neither Simon nor the duke would pay for a new overpass, and every time she crossed the rickety planks during flood season, her nerves tightened taut as harp strings. The stream wasn't more than four or five feet deep, but the rushing water frightened her nevertheless.

She couldn't swim. Not a stroke.

After falling from the dock and nearly drowning as a six-year-old, she'd acquired a tremendous fear of water.

That was why she usually took the other, newer bridge. This track was much closer to Perygrim Park however, and with the weather about to express her displeasure, and considering Mama's episode this morning, Eden couldn't take the time to detour to the other crossing.

"My lord, perhaps your first duty could be to

replace, or at the very least, repair this bridge? Simon refuses to pay for it, as does the duke, and passage becomes more unstable with each crossing. I fear the worst for an unsuspecting traveler."

A stiff draught whipped several strands of hair around her shoulders, and she shook her head to fling them from her face.

While at school, she'd endured people's unkind staring and pointing, other girls whispering and some even calling the brownish red patch on her neck a devil's mark or witch's kiss. She'd rather deal with the unruly tresses than the unkindness and curious stares.

"Consider it done, Miss Haverden. Now as to that other matter." Lord Sterling laid one arm across the back of the seat and presented his noble profile. "I've been away for a decade and wouldn't be here now except my sire is gravely ill. Plainly put, I'm an outsider now, and I could use a friend."

A friend?

So could she, truth to tell.

Though Newbury's citizens treated her kindly, she fit neither with the commoners nor with the local gentry. Not outwardly shunned, neither was she included in social gatherings or assemblies. Except for those hosted by Vicar Jedidiah Wright.

Six weeks ago, he'd proposed for the fourth time.

He was to be commended for his persistence, even if she never intended to accept his offer.

Caring, gentle, and attractive in his quiet reserved way, and a widower with two small children, Vicar Wright couldn't fathom why anyone should mind if he took a bastard to wife. His love for humanity and his non-judgmental soul were blind to the censured looks parishioners cast him whenever he spoke with Eden.

She truly feared if she accepted, he might well lose his position.

The last time her brother Simon had threatened to evict them, Eden had seriously considered Vicar Wright's proposal. In the end, she couldn't bring herself to say yes, even if it meant an assurance Mama would have somewhere to live.

Despite her conscience pealing an alarm, she met Lord Sterling's inquisitive gaze.

My, he had the loveliest eyes. She could get quite

lost in their intriguing depths.

Rogue or gentleman?

What did it matter?

She'd already made up her mind.

An innocent friendship. Nothing more.

There couldn't be.

"I should like that, my lord, as well. As long as we stay well within propriety's strictures."

That ought to make her position clear.

"Might you consider addressing me as Chester when we are alone?"

Brow cocked, she gave him a starchy glance.

Was he testing the limits already?

"You know perfectly well that's outside the bounds."

He chuckled, a wonderful raffish echo in that chest she knew to be nicely muscled. When the wheels hit an uneven board and jostled the cart, he gripped the seat. Probably not used to having his manly bum bounced about.

"It is," he said. "But friends are permitted privileges, are they not?"

"I suppose they are. But only small concessions."

Shushing her conscience's frenetic warnings about foolhardy decisions, she returned his easy-going grin. For the briefest instant. Then a startled gasp tore from her fear-constricted throat.

"Oh, no!"

The eerie crack of first one plank, then another, and then another rent the moist air and stalled her breathing. If the dogcart spilled into the churning stream-turned-river, Mr. Wiggles and Peony might drown.

So might she and his lordship.

"Get off, my lord. Now!"

Eden released the reins and scampered from the wagon as did Lord Sterling without a jot of hesitation

"Help me push." Neither very big nor strong, she couldn't budge the vehicle on her own. "We must get the wheel free. Hurry."

He positioned his shoulder behind the cart, tension accenting the slashing angles of his cheeks.

"Walk on, Peony, walk on," she shouted whilst giving the cart another hard shove.

The caught wheel suddenly came loose and bounced forward.

Unbalanced, arms flailing, and her heart pounding in her throat, she tottered backward.

Then . . . off the bridge.

"Eden!"

A torrent of freezing water engulfed her, and she struggled against the weight of her saturated cloak and gown. Terror momentarily paralyzed her. A panic-born burst of energy assailed her, and she fought in vain to reach the surface just a couple of feet above her.

It might as well have been a score.

The relentless current yanked and tugged, forcing her head under again and again.

She choked and gasped, seeking purchase on something, anything, to gain her footing and lift her face from the pummeling.

Time slowed, inching forward, the roaring in her ears growing ever louder and more insistent.

Her hair caught, jerking her head so sharply, she cried out. Rushing water promptly filled her mouth and lungs. The unbearable pressure in her chest crushed her lungs.

3

Purplish blackness engulfed Eden just as vice-like hands seized her beneath the armpits and unceremoniously hauled her against a solid form whilst dragging her toward the embankment.

"I've got you, Eden," A deep, velvety warm voice rasped in her ear. "I've got you. Don't be afraid. You're safe now."

Lord Sterling?

Stiff from fear and cold, her icy limbs dead weight, she couldn't lift a finger in assistance. A tiny, frightened whimper made it past her clamped jaw.

"Just a little farther," he grated, his breath ragged and labored. "Stay with me, sweet."

What a delicious notion. If only such a thing were possible.

Then he plopped her onto the shore, dropped to his knees and brushed his hands over her face, patting her cheeks. Tilting her head, he pressed his firm mouth to hers and blew.

Mmm, that's rather nice.

He pressed hard on her chest.

Ow. Not nearly as pleasant.

A second powerful push. And a third.

Ouch. Not so hard.

She rolled to her side and vomited.

"That's it. Get all the water out."

Scraping sopping strands of hair from her face, he cradled her body against his splendid warmth.

Sweet God, she was mortified, not to mention freezing cold.

She wanted to climb on top of his lordship, burrow into his warm, fabulous smelling chest, and stay there until her limbs thawed. Shaking from toe to head, she clenched her teeth to halt their chattering. After a few moments, she forced her lids open, her gaze melding with Lord Sterling's gentle yet arresting eyes.

"You frightened a decade off my life. I shan't be surprised to find I've gone quite gray."

He tipped his lips upward as he traced her cheek with his fingertip.

"Please tell me you're all right, Eden."

Groaning, she gingerly fingered her throbbing scalp. "My head . . ."

She coughed, clutching at her aching chest, and closed her eyes once more.

Using two fingers, she probed the tender spot at the base of her skull.

"I'm to blame for your head. You were being dragged downstream so fast, I grabbed your hair to stop you."

Eyes still shut, she managed a wobbly smile.

"So being unfashionable saved my life, it seems."

"Indeed."

He chuckled, the sound resonating with relief, yet still held her tight to his chest. She made no effort to move away from the wonderful feeling.

She did manage to crack her eyelids open.

Mouth turned down, worry crinkling the edges of his eyes, he examined her scalp. The merest stubble darkened his carved jaw.

"You're not bleeding, but I imagine you'll be sore for a few days. I am truly sorry, but I was desperate to prevent you from drowning."

"I also almost drowned when I was six."

Why she thought to volunteer that at this moment, she couldn't say.

His lordship hugged her tighter, those marvelous strong arms making her feel safe.

"Poor darling. This must've been all the more terrifying."

A high-pitched cry and a hard nudge from a wet doggy nose announced Mr. Wiggle's arrival. His muddy front paws on Lord Sterling's wet, marble-like thigh, he anxiously sniffed her face, then licked her cheek, whining the whole while.

"I'm fine, Mr. Wiggles."

Well, perhaps not fine. She hurt all over and probably would be bruised worse than an apple used to play conkers. Her throat burned as if she'd swallowed hot coals, and her lungs ached something fierce, as if fiery little needles were poking non-stop. But, thanks to Lord Sterling still embracing her and soaked to the skin as well, she was alive.

Somehow, he managed to awkwardly stand while drawing her upward. Weak and exhausted, her knees soft as flummery, she leaned heavily against him.

Sturdy as a tree trunk, he didn't waver under her weight.

"We need to get you warm before you catch lung fever. Perygrim is just there."

He dipped his dripping head toward the mansion's austere silhouette.

"Impossible, my lord." Eden shook her head, cloying strands of hair clinging to her neck and face. "I'm not allowed—"

"I'll hear no more about that nonsense." A harshness she'd never heard before made his tone flint-like. "You wouldn't have almost drowned if you hadn't been doing me a kindness. The least I can do is see you safely bathed, tucked into a warm bed, and fed hot soup and perhaps a toddy as well."

After scooping her into his arms, he effortlessly strode to the cart, now safely standing on the other side of the bridge.

She tried a different tack. One Lord Sterling couldn't argue against.

"But my mother—"

"I shall send a note explaining what's happened and tell her that if you are fully recovered, I'll escort you home tomorrow."

So much for not trespassing upon propriety.

He bundled Eden onto the seat, resting his broad hand upon her shoulder.

"Are you able to sit up on your own, or should I put you in the wagon bed?"

"I . . . can . . . manage," she stuttered between her chattering teeth.

Even her marrow throbbed from the cold tunneling through her. Truly, the idea of waiting until she reached Briar Knoll to finally remove her saturated clothing convinced her he was right. She'd have to prepare her own bath and doubted she had the strength to do so.

The sun's remnants had disappeared below the horizon, and the breeze had developed into a full-on wind. Their branches swaying in the murky twilight, the trees swished and groaned. Any hope of making Perygrim before the clouds spilled their contents vanished as the first few heavy drops splattered from above a moment before the flood poured forth.

The striking lines and planes of his face, which bespoke generations of nobility, grew stern as Lord Sterling retrieved his greatcoat from beside the wagon. After settling Mr. Wiggles in the wagon bed, he leaped onto the cart, then wrapped his overcoat around Eden's shoulders before pulling her to his side and draping one arm around her shoulders.

Such an intimate thing to do, and she didn't mind this infringement one iota.

"My coat should stay the wind a bit."

"Thank you, but you'll be cold now. It's very gallant of you."

Peculiar shyness blanketed her, and she fought the impulse to turn her gaze away.

Humor softened his mouth as he assumed a

courtier's pose, one hand pressed to his chest and chiseled chin elevated.

"Hark, fear not, fair maiden. Chivalry shall warm my unworthy flesh, and knowing my humble covering bringest thou a measure of comfort kindles a fire in my blood."

"Fire in your blood? Sounds terribly painful to me."

More physically miserable than she could ever recall, from whence she summoned her droll humor, she didn't know. But his chivalry had earned him a high mark in her esteem.

Lowering her chin the merest bit, she touched her nose to the coat and inhaled. The garment smelled of his lordship—the aroma comforting and sensual at the same time. She ought to object to his forwardness. That would be the proper thing to do. At this juncture, honestly, she was so dratted cold and uncomfortable, she didn't give a chicken's tail feather about decorum.

Her earlier consternation about whether he was a knave or an honorable man had been answered, but she'd suspected as much all along.

"I don't think you'll need to polish your boots after all," she quipped, boldly pressing into his body's heat.

Wisdom decreed she continue on to Briar Knoll after delivering Lord Sterling to Perygrim. The impropriety of what he'd suggested hadn't escaped her, even if he meant nothing untoward.

Quickly calculating how long it would take to deliver him home and then continue on in the dark—by herself—to the cottage in this ever-increasing foul weather, made her slump her shoulders.

Close to a half hour. Mayhap more.

She'd catch her death.

But was staying at Perygrim a lesser risk?

She forced her mind to a different topic.

"Just send a note round with the amount I owe you for your garments and boots." Shuddering, she pressed her lips together and hunched deeper into his heavy coat.

Lord Sterling laughed, really laughed. The pleasant peal resounded in his chest.

"I most assuredly will not. On the other hand, your

clothes might be ruined on account of our detour, and I must insist on replacing them."

No. *He* would not.

The gossipmongers would swarm around that like flies on dead fish. She was flirting with ruin as it was.

Less than ten minutes later, night almost fully upon them, he guided the cart down the tidy stone drive to stop before the imposing manor.

Peony expressed her displeasure with a wicker and flick of her tail. She wanted her warm stall at Briar Knoll.

Craning her neck, Eden surveyed the stately house.

Perygrim seemed lonely, almost forlorn. The impressive entry door swung open, and a bland-faced majordomo appeared in the illumined entrance. His contempt palatable, he peered down his nose.

"I believe you are lost. We are not expecting guests, nor is his grace home to anyone."

"Come now, Wynby. Have I truly changed that much?"

Lord Sterling handed her down and, keeping his

fingers on her elbow, guided her toward the squinting butler.

"My lord?" A joyous smile transformed the fusty fellow in a trice. "It is truly you?"

"I said I'd be home for my birthday, and here I am.

A welcoming, almost boyish smile curving his mouth, his lordship gestured wide with both arms.

"It's your birthday today?" This was even worse. She was intruding on a family celebration. She stopped and faced him. Voice lowered, she said, "I cannot possibly impose."

Perhaps she could borrow a blanket and a lantern for her miserable trek home.

"Yes, it is," Lord Sterling said, "and of course you can. You are my guest. I shall brook no refusal."

Before she had an opportunity to summon a suitable response or become vexed at his high-handed methods, he'd bustled her straight to the beaming butler.

"Wynby, this is Miss Eglantina Haverden. She prefers Miss Eden. She graciously offered me a ride home when my horse went lame in Newbury. But as you've probably already surmised, we had a bit of a mishap. The old bridge gave way, she nearly drowned, and we're both nigh on to freezing."

Not exactly true. Part of the bridge had collapsed, and in her ungainliness, she had tumbled into the brook.

"I should say so, sir. That span has been a worry for some time now. Not to fret. We'll have baths prepared at once. Dinner isn't until seven, so you've plenty of time to bathe and dress. Your trunks arrived two days ago, and your valet has already unpacked them." Pressing his palms together, the middle-aged servant practically bounced in his excitement. "Cook has prepared a treat for you. Beef Wellington and trifle."

You'd have thought he'd announced the Prince Regent was to dine with them, such was his proud satisfaction.

"See," Lord Sterling whispered in her ear. "Nothing flusters the unflappable Wynby. We could have arrived naked as cherubs, and he wouldn't have blinked."

When he said naked, she flashed hot and cold. Or maybe it was his warm breath caressing her ear that caused the onslaught.

Whatever was wrong with her?

For certain, a fever couldn't have set in yet. Could it have?

"The young lady will have to wear something belonging to one of the maids." Eyeing Eden up and down, concern pinched the butler's full mouth. "I apologize, Miss Eden. No offense is intended, I promise you. There are simply no other females in the household."

No others? Not even a housekeeper or cook?

She closed her eyes and swallowed. What had she gotten herself into? If word got out . . .

"Mrs. Gibbs and Mrs. Lackman are no longer at Perygrim?"

So, Lord Sterling hadn't been aware either?

Wynby shook his head.

His lordship brushed his crooked forefinger along his upper lip, the causal movement at odds with the thoughtful sternness in his eyes.

"They retired within a month of each other last year, my lord, and went to live with their daughters. We haven't had a housekeeper since, but Monsieur Fournier took Cook's position. *He* is French."

That stiff-lipped pronouncement said much.

She had no choice. To stay was to invite ruin, and when you were already outside of propriety's boundaries, that wasn't a risk to take lightly.

"Lord Sterling, though I do appreciate your noble intentions, my reputation will be in shreds should I stay the night without a female companion."

Not to mention what the gossip would do to Mama if she heard it.

More on point and of equal concern was Simon. What if he got wind of her imprudence? He'd be in a right high dudgeon.

"Forgive my boldness, but I'm sure one of the downstairs maids wouldn't mind sharing your chamber and acting the part of a chaperone," Wynby offered. "The rose bedchamber has a divan the maid can sleep on, and the room locks from within."

"Is that satisfactory?" His lordship searched her face, worry tautening his already angular features. "I fear your health will suffer if you remain in those wet clothes."

As did she.

Eden was a woman full grown after all—on the shelf, truth be told—and quite capable of making rational decisions. It wasn't as if she was spending the night in a house of ill-repute. She hurt all over, and a merciless cadence ticked between her temples.

Pulling Lord Sterling's greatcoat more securely about her shoulders, she tried to ignore the rivulets running down her neck and under the collar.

"That is more than satisfactory. All I require is something to sleep in. I'll lay my clothes out to dry, so no one needs to trouble with them on my behalf."

From the cart, Mr. Wiggles gave a worried woof.

Poor dear. He was just as wet and miserable.

"My lord, what about my dog? He's never been away from me."

His lordship whistled, and at once, Mr. Wiggles jumped from the wagon and bounded to his side.

"He'll come with us and dry himself before the fire in your room. I'm sure Cook can muster tasty scraps for the handsome fellow too."

What a load of blather. Mr. Wiggles was ugly. Plain and simple. But he had the most loyal, beautiful heart, and that's what she saw when she looked at him. Not his mangy, scruffy outward trappings.

Reluctant, and quivering from cold, she permitted Lord Sterling to lead her into the house. A tomb held more warmth and was more welcoming. No wonder he'd avoided the place for a decade.

"I shan't dine with you and intrude upon your reunion with your father. I'd prefer to be shown a room at once, and I'll eat there," she said, with unwavering firmness.

Besides, she'd rather be at her best if and when she met his grace, not grass-and mud-caked with her hair hanging in straggly tendrils.

The prudent thing to do would be to leave at once, but the truth of it was she felt rather awful. Better to stay here, tucked into a warm bed, than risk becoming stranded on the way home, or worse yet, finding she was too weak after all to make it home.

She might not know Lord Sterling well, but he wasn't the sort to let her traipse home by herself, she'd be bound. Which meant he'd have to miss his birthday dinner.

Perhaps it wasn't quite *de rigueur*, but surely with a maid in attendance and the door securely locked, no one could suggest anything improper had occurred. Even with a note delivered to explain what had waylaid Eden, Mama would fuss. Naught could be done about that unfortunateness.

His lordship opened his mouth, likely to object, but she stalled him with a short shake of her head and uplifted hand.

Lovely. Dirt smeared her fingers and caked her nails.

"I must insist, my lord. I'm honestly not feeling myself just yet."

With a gracious inclination of his wet head, the candlelight giving his hair the aura of burnished copper, Lord Sterling conceded.

"Yes, perhaps straight to bed is the best plan. I

would hate for you to fall ill." He lifted her hand and kissed the dirty knuckles, and her dratted insides went all melty.

More butterflies flitted from her knees to her chest, then circled round and round in her middle. How could she be so taken with a man she'd only just met?

"I'll see you in the morning then," he said. "Should you need anything, don't hesitate to ring. Wynby and the other staff are at your service. Isn't that so, Wynby?"

"Indeed, we are available for your every need, Miss." Perhaps a tinge less enthusiasm weighted the butler's words as he looked over his shoulder to the hallway beyond.

"Is that my wayward son at last?" a feeble male voice called.

Oh, no.

The opportunity to escape without meeting his grace had vanished.

"Neville, you feeble-minded bacon brain, take me to him at once," the same crackly elderly voice demanded. "Where's Dockery? He is never about when I need him. I told him to await my son's homecoming. Stop dawdling and shuffling along like a pregnant cow, Neville, for God sake. Cannot you push this blasted chair any faster? Move, you ham-fisted puff guts."

His harsh demands plucked at Eden's already frayed nerves, and she raised her appalled gaze to his lordship. No wonder his grace had such a wretched reputation.

Did he always speak thusly to his staff?

A disgusted smirk arching his mouth, his eyes gone slate, Lord Sterling elevated a mocking brow.

"My father always has had an eloquent way with words and knows no shortage of colorful insults."

The wheels of an invalid-chair whirred in the corridor, and then the notorious Duke of DeCourcy, the Demon Duke, appeared. A shriveled, wasted shell of a man with sparse white hair, red-rimmed, puffy bagged eyes beneath a scowl fierce enough to send the devil himself into hiding. Yet in the architecture of his face and his unusual colored eyes, there was no mistaking his kinship to Lord Sterling.

"Father."

Expression unreadable, his lordship dipped his head respectfully, but Eden didn't miss his taut mouth or stiff shoulders.

Not a loving homecoming, by any means.

The duke's watery gaze, scornful and contemptuous, swerved to Eden. He thrust his bony jaw forward and pounded his gnarled hands upon the chair's arms.

"By God, you have bloody-damn nerve, Manchester."

She cringed at the rancor radiating from his grace. This was a huge mistake. She turned to tell Lord Sterling as much again, but he halted her with a commanding look. Much more went on here than an uninvited guest's imposition.

This was a battle between two stags, the old sickly animal not willing to relinquish his position, and the new determined that it be so.

Though his features remained impassive, she didn't miss the spark of anger flashing in his lordship's eyes.

"I'll thank you to refrain from cursing with a lady present, Father."

"*Phsaw*. Lady my arse." His grace made a curt, sweeping gesture and leaned forward, his lips curled into a snarl. "You've so little respect for me and the duchy that you've brought your strumpet to this noble house?"

Something dangerous, almost sinister flexed across Lord Sterling's face.

"Sir, you cross the mark. Miss Eden is my *guest*, and I insist she be treated with the respect due her."

"I'll just go." Eden said as she removed his coat from her shoulders. "Home is not so very far."

It only seemed so. In the dark. During a downpour. When she was already saturated and quaking with cold.

Nonetheless, she was determined to leave. A vile, palatable thing, the duke's animosity stretched the distance across the entry, its tentacles coiling around her and squeezing the air from her lungs.

She turned to depart, but Lord Sterling's firm hand on her elbow halted her.

"No. You shan't. You will stay."

A command. Not a request.

Unrelenting steeliness made each syllable clipped, but it was the flint-like resolve in his eyes, almost pewter gray with controlled ire, that he speared his sire that shushed her protest.

A test of wills.

If staying meant Lord Sterling won this round against his devilish father, then by Jupiter, Eden would stay.

"Wait." The duke clawed at his rumpled neckcloth, his face an unhealthy pallor. "Demme. Is she . . .? No, by all that's holy. You would not dare."

The old man's mouth worked, and for a moment, she thought he might be in the throes of an apoplectic fit.

She swallowed as every eye focused on her, and for the first time in a great while, humiliation and mortification sluiced through her, heating her cheeks. Head tilted at a proud angle, she didn't flinch from his grace's caustic scrutiny.

"That's . . . That's Andrew's bastard." Face

contorted in disbelief and bony fingers clutching the chair arms, he trembled with rage. "You have the gall to bring Satan's spawn here? Into my house? When you know how I feel about those . . . those *maggots*?"

"Father . . ." Holding himself rigid, his lordship strode to the duke. Towering over the shrunken man, he visibly fought to control his ire. "Make no mistake. Insult Miss Eden again, and I'll leave Perygrim this very night. And I shall never return whilst you yet breathe."

That took the wind out of the old man's sails.

His grace collapsed into his chair, and mouth pressed into a pout, arranged his drooping blanket across his spindly thighs. The smile he formed as he raked Eden with his hostile gaze was nothing short of evil. Full of malicious satisfaction as well.

"Fornicate all you want with the drab then, but in a month Viscountess Bickford and her charming daughter arrive for a week-long house party at Perygrim. Lady Bickford assures me Gabriella will make an exceptional duchess. I expect you to honor my pledge that you'll take her to wife. Do your duty to the dukedom by proposing before the party is over."

4

Sitting at the breakfast table the next morning, Chester glanced at his watch for the third time as he drank his coffee. Would Eden come down, or had his father succeeded in thoroughly terrifying her?

Five more minutes, then he'd go find her himself.

He'd wanted to bid her good night but couldn't conceive of any rational excuse to knock upon her door at half past ten. As it was, it had taken a full hour to calm his sire into any semblance of reason. Chester had finally resorted to threatening to leave at once if she and Mr. Wiggles weren't permitted to stay and shown the respect he required.

Much to his father's consternation, he'd refused to

even discuss the ridiculousness of a credible match with Miss Gabriella Bickford. She might be a beauty and an heir to a vulgarly large banking fortune as well as the sizable estate one county over, and the few times Chester had been in her company, she seemed to have a sensible head upon her dainty white shoulders. But hounds' teeth, the duke wasn't going to dictate who he married.

He'd made Mother a promise and, if possible, he intended to keep it. But then again, surely his mother must have realized how difficult love—real, sacrificial love—was to find, and even more so how a man in his position was expected to wed for profit and gain, not sentimental claptrap as Father called the emotion.

Naturally, she had.

Because she'd done just that.

Married the ruthless, titled, significantly older peer her parents had selected, bringing her own fortune to the union and regrettably, her naive hopes and girlish dreams as well.

For a moment, he let his eyelids drift shut, remembering his shy, sweet-tempered mother. She'd been no match for the fierce duke's darkling temper, his unrepentant whoring and drinking, or his barbed cruelty. Two years after removing herself to The Lake Cottage, she'd died. Broken and disillusioned, but not before exacting a promise from Chester.

"Marry for love, Chester darling. Naught else matters or endures. Promise me, son."

Adoring her, he had, of course.

Too bad he couldn't abdicate his responsibilities and engage in another pursuit during the house party. Father had invited forty of *le beau monde's* most influential and prestigious denizens for the gathering. Probably half that number included cow-eyed ingénues eager to snare a duke.

Damn my eyes.

He brushed a hand across those suddenly very weary orbs.

If he was to rejuvenate the duchy's tainted reputation, he couldn't snub the guests by removing himself to London for the farce's duration.

Stretching his legs, he yawned and surveyed the comfortable room before pouring more coffee.

Mother's touch yet remained from the cheerful jonquil and indigo silk wall coverings—now faded with age—to the floral damask covered chairs and the Blue Fluted china, used for serving breakfast. Unlike when his mother was alive, a fine coating of dust covered the sideboard and windowsills. The knick-knacks too.

Last evening, he'd noticed other signs of neglect. The great house and her grounds had seen better days. While some of the negligence might be blamed on Father's ill health and lack of oversight, Chester suspected something more disturbing might be afoot. Not all the servants possessed a work ethic such as Wynby's.

Sighing, Chester steered his thoughts to a more optimistic vein.

He and Eden would have the charming breakfast room to themselves this morning. Neville had confided that Father slept poorly most nights and relied upon laudanum to find any degree of rest. He seldom awoke before noon. Dockery, Father's man—thug better described the cur—had claimed when he met Chester in the corridor this morning that he had important business to attend in Newbury.

Fearful his father might set Dockery on some mischievous task, Chester had stationed himself outside Eden's chamber for the night. His back ached from the crick caused by slumping in the high back chair for hours.

Just what were Dockery's duties anyway?

Far past time he was dismissed without reference, which Chester fully intended to do once he'd made a thorough inspection of the accounts, correspondences, and ledgers.

Just as well Eden had declined to eat dinner with him last night. Not only would his sire have treated her abominably, the old tosspot had done nothing but complain, harangue Neville, and pretty much attempt to make everyone as miserable as he.

After a decade, Chester had anticipated that perhaps Father had mellowed, had stopped being so corrosive and toxic—had stopped loathing the Andrews.

Not a bit of it.

If anything, the passage of time had intensified Father's malice. That was what happened when men grew old and had nothing else to occupy themselves with. They ruminated, their ugly musings becoming as rotten as a festering wound, distorting their reason. Bitterness warped a person's mind if they wallowed in it day in and day out.

That hadn't stopped Chester from telling his sire, in the bluntest of terms, that he was never to cause any sort of harm to Eden, nor disrespect her in any fashion again, unless he wanted Chester to leave at once. He'd stalked from the dining room, his father hurling raspy curses at his retreating back.

Happy birthday, and welcome home.

This afternoon, Father had an appointment with a new physician, hired by Chester in London, and he anticipated a full accounting of his father's health issues. He'd already sent word to the bailiff that he wanted a meeting at his earliest convenience to go over the estate's operations and accounts as well. From what he'd seen of the books last night, Dockery wasn't the only employee taking advantage of Father's ill health.

A small sigh escaped him before he took a sip of the strong coffee sweetened with two sugar lumps.

Why had he expected anything to have changed?

Father blamed him for Byron's death. He'd made that abundantly clear last night. It did rather scrape nastily to know Chester's sire wished him dead so his brother might be alive.

If it weren't for his confounded duty to the duchy, he'd be away today. Nothing else held him here.

Captivating blue eyes danced across his mind.

Well, there was that intriguing female upstairs he'd like to become further acquainted with.

Once he'd determined everything was in order and consulted with the physician, he'd make a decision about whether to stay on. Residing in the same house as his sire after all these years he couldn't do.

Not yet.

Mayhap not ever.

He'd already asked to have his possessions moved to The Lake Cottage. Which, luckily for him and his fascination with a certain azure-eyed nymph, was directly across Lake Blackton from Briar Cottage. If he stood on the dock a short distance from the house, he could see the windows of Eden's home.

His attention gravitated to the doorway again.

She still hadn't come down.

Was she unwell?

Unease swept him, and he straightened as he set his cup down.

Why hadn't he considered that before?

Fool.

He should've insisted she be examined by a physician last night. She might be feverish, fighting lung fever, unable to call for help. Or afraid to after her hostile reception last night.

Tossing his serviette on his plate, Chester shoved his chair back. A movement beyond the window caught his attention, and he whirled to face the drive.

Her long hair skimming her behind, Eden rattled along in her dogcart. A serene Mr. Wiggles sat beside her as they rolled down the driveway.

Without a farewell.

How could he blame her when his father had

called her a whore upon their first meeting?

Chester had almost said, "For shame, Father, she's not any such thing. She's the future Duchess of DeCourcy."

Where such an obscure notion had risen from, he couldn't fathom. He wasn't given to rash impulses. He'd refrained mostly because Father might've expired on the spot, and even with as much discord as there was between them, Chester didn't want the albatross of causing the duke's death on his conscience. Besides, unlike his sire, he didn't stoop to deliberate cruelty, and he'd never put Eden in such an awkward position.

His concern for her health had been genuine. In retrospect, insisting she stay last night mightn't have been the wisest of choices.

Nevertheless . . .

Chester wrenched open the French windows leading to what was once his mother's immaculately attended rose gardens. Pelting across the weed-choked stepping-stones, all the while waving his arms in a manner befitting a rambunctious child, he called her name.

"Miss Eden, please wait."

Even to his ears, he sounded frantic.

Just like a love-struck swain.

She turned her head and gifted him with one of her incredible smiles over her shoulder.

The queer fluttering behind his breastbone couldn't be entirely blamed on his bullish dash from the house.

"I was told you were meeting with your bailiff, my lord. Else I would've said good-bye in person. I left a note with Wynby thanking you and the duke for your hospitality."

Her manners remained impeccable despite Father's unforgiveable behavior.

Chester caught up to her, and resting his forearm on the cart's edge, grinned. Only she had the ability to make him smile like a trained monkey. Didn't she know he had a reputation to maintain as the formidable Marquis of Sterling?

"Who told you that codswallop? My appointment with Jervis isn't until this afternoon."

He'd wager he knew full well who had. Dockery,

the sour-faced sot. Chester intended to dismiss him right after discharging Jervis. That meant he had to hire a secretary and steward, in addition to a housekeeper. From what he'd seen of the grounds, another gardener wouldn't be amiss either.

"Oh, well. It matters naught. I need to get home promptly in any event. Mama will be fretting despite the note that was sent. I've not been gone overnight since she took ill." She plucked a dog hair from her clean cinnamon colored gown.

Someone must have seen to Eden's garments last night. Probably Wynby's thoughtfulness, done on Chester's behalf. Byron might've been Father's favorite, probably because he was just like him, but as a gangly lad, Chester had won the hearts of his dear departed mother and Perygrim's staff.

While Eden looked fetching in her simple attire, her eyes and soft tawny hair truly lent themselves to softer hues. Pale greens, pinks, sky-blue. Now those were the shades for her. Spring colors.

"Might I accompany you?" he asked

The words left his mouth before he could stop

them. What was it about her that made him yearn to be with her? What had him casting aside his usual decorum, discipline and vigilance, and brushing aside his duties? They'd met less than twenty-four hours ago, yet he felt as if his spirit knew hers.

Blister and ballocks.

He was the daunting Lord Sterling. Not a mewling wet-behind-the ears milksop prone to fanciful balderdash.

"Given the duke's reaction last evening, are you certain that would be altogether wise, my lord?"

Was she troubled for him?

"He'd best get used to it. Besides, I thought perhaps you might show me your herbs. I would like our chef to purchase those he needs from you in future. If you have a sufficient supply, that is. Perhaps we could buy honey too? I'm quite fond of quince with honey and nuts."

A finger on her small chin, Eden tilted her head. After a prolonged moment of her intelligent gaze searching his eyes, probing his very soul, she gave a short nod.

"I have a quince tree too, but they won't be ripe for months yet."

He'd seen the reservation in her eyes, seen her mind chugging away, trying to decide if she could trust him. Likely, she'd spent her entire life assessing people in that manner, never quite sure who was friend or foe.

Because she lived between two worlds, fitting into neither, and destined to be an outsider.

Not quite suitable for gentry or *haut ton* parlors, but neither was she accepted in the lower orders. How difficult her life must be. Judged by everyone for no fault of hers, struggling to find her place in an unkind world. She was resourceful though. He'd learned that much about her in their short acquaintance.

Eggs, honey, herbs.

What else did Eglantina Haverden dabble in?

As he climbed aboard the cart, she tugged Mr. Wiggles closer.

Chester didn't miss her slight wince. No doubt she was sore from her unfortunate escapade.

Yesterday's petulant weather had blown through,

and a vivid azure sky, with an occasional cottony cloud scattered here and there, had taken its place. A hedgerow, heavy with pink buds, bordered one side of the drive. They'd be bursting into bloom soon, as would the overgrown roses he'd just tramped through.

She hummed and tapped her little feet while she drove. Beyond a doubt, she was the most unpretentious, unabashed woman he'd ever met. Unlike most ladies of his acquaintance, she didn't seem to feel the need to jabber on about nonsensical things.

He studied her pert profile from her straight, little slightly turned-up nose to her adorable chin.

There was something truly unique about Miss Eden Haverden.

She'd studiously avoided mentioning Gabriella Bickford, and he wasn't broaching that prickly subject either. Just because his father had commanded it, that didn't mean Chester would concede to the alliance.

Content just to be near Eden, he surveyed Perygrim's lands. Until this very minute, he hadn't realized how much he'd yearned to see these very fields and woods again. Or row a boat across Lake Blackton and swim in it too. Naked as the day he was born, just as he and Byron used to do as youths.

Peony clopped along, her ridiculous hat and silk flowers bobbing with each footstep. What had Perygrim's grooms made of the accessory? He'd like to have been a barn cat curled in a nest of hay and listened to that conversation.

"Just yonder," he pointed to a pine stand, "is where the huge stag was downed that spurred the argument between your brother and mine. They fought the duel in that meadow to the right."

Why he felt the need to address that matter, he couldn't rightly say. Her brother had killed his, yet Chester felt no animosity toward her.

Why should he? She'd had no part in the feud, which had been fought fairly.

He most assuredly meant to see to it this dispute ended, but as with any disagreement, all parties must be amenable to reconciliation.

He doubted his sire would ever waver in his hatred toward the Andrews.

"I'd heard a little about what caused the rift, but not the whole story. There wasn't anyone I could ask. My siblings refuse to speak of it, not that I ever inquired directly. And I shan't resort to rumor-mongering in the village. A story told second-hand is rarely accurate, I've found."

She shifted, adjusting her legs, and her mouth twitched in pleasure as a squirrel dashed across the lane.

"You'll get to meet Acorn too. She's my pet squirrel. I rescued her when the oak where her nest lay was felled. She didn't even have her eyes open yet. I fed her with a pipette."

Why didn't it surprise him in the least that Eden had a pet squirrel? Probably had a pet pig named Petunia, a milk cow named Daisy, and half a dozen cats with rhyming names like Suzette, Minette, Annette, and Bridgette. He'd be bound she named her chickens too.

"My lord, you needn't explain if it upsets you."

Ten long years ago, and yet as they juddered past the glen, every detail was as fresh as if Byron had died yesterday.

Staring at the trees, at the very place where his brother's blood had drained from him, Chester sighed in remembered pain and frustration.

Manchester, it should've been you who was shot.

You!

Not your brother.

Byron was to have been the duke.

Why didn't you challenge Andrews in his stead, you poltroon? You were the spare.

Clasping Byron to his chest, the duke had sobbed, *Oh, my beloved son.*

"In truth, both our brothers shot the stag," Chester said.

"Both of them?"

Her swift glance contained surprise and uncertainty. She touched two fingers to her forehead and closed her eyes for an instant.

"Eden, are you all right?"

"Yes, yes. Fine. I've a slight headache, that's all. Probably from the sun."

More likely from him dragging her from the

stream by her hair.

A chagrined smile quirked her lips up on one side. "Mama is forever scolding me for not wearing a bonnet, but yesterday's weather required my cloak hood. Much more practical and far warmer than a hat."

Was she always sensible?

"Tell me more about that day our brothers dueled, if you wouldn't mind. Perhaps I can better understand the rift between our families."

"I don't mind, but the tale's not pleasant."

He closed his eyes, picturing the brisk fall morning they'd gone stalking. Frost iced the grass and shimmered in the spiders' webs. Crisp leaves in shades of brown, gold, and burgundy had crunched beneath their boots. Cheeks whipped red by the autumn wind and fingers stiff from cold, impatient to find their quarry, the trio had separated from the rest of the more sedate hunting party.

Lord, the stag had been a magnificent beast standing betwixt the trunks, his noble head lifted, such wisdom in his knowing umber-eyed gaze.

"I had him in my sights as well. I saw everything.

Only I couldn't pull the trigger. Such a majestic creature ought to have been allowed to live. To die of old age in these woods." He waved a hand, indicating the woodlands they rumbled past. "I've no doubt his offspring yet roam the meadows and copses."

"I'm sure you are right. I have several deer that visit my orchard every morning. Their gentle beauty never fails to affect me. Once in a great while, I'll feed them a little cracked corn, but I can ill afford to do so daily."

No self-pity colored her voice, just the stark frankness that had marked all of their conversations.

Cutting him a sideways glance, she scrunched her forehead, her confusion evident. "So, what happened to cause so much ill-will that a stalking adventure became an affair of honor?"

"Simon and Byron fired at almost the exact same moment. There wasn't any way to know which shot actually killed the stag. He was such a strong animal, I've often thought it took both to down him."

That day, Chester had forsworn hunting forever.

Two grown men squabbling like intractable

children over who slayed an unsuspecting stag. Not because they needed the meat, but because they coveted the superb antlers. Each had wanted to be the man to boast about his great hunting feat. As if killing a defenseless animal for sport made them some sort of hero.

Empathy softened Eden's features as she peered across the expanse.

"They should've let him live." For a moment, her tender gaze caressed his face, and welcoming warmth spiraled upward from his belly. "I'd vow you tried to tell them what you saw, and they refused to hear it. Their pride and arrogance prevented them from considering you were right. That same pride and arrogance led to the stupid duel too, didn't it?"

For an instant, he sat dumfounded.

She understood.

"Indeed, it did. Byron, always hot-headed and ready to take offense at the least perceived slight, issued the challenge. Neither would listen to reason, however. He named me his second, and I could do naught but agree in the hope I could persuade him to settle the matter another way. The duel was only to have been to first blood."

Chester pulled his cuff down even as the scene played out in his mind again, as it had too many times to count over the years. Inevitably, he asked himself the same critical question: Was there anything he could have done to save Byron's life?

Expertly steering the old cart to the right of a large puddle, Eden crinkled her forehead again. Every time she did that, the mark on her forehead twitched.

"But, if it was only to first blood, then how . . .?"

"Your brother had first shot. He aimed to Byron's right, but our father arrived and shouted for them to stop. My brother panicked and tried to leap out of the way. Instead, he dove right into the line of fire. Nothing could be done. The wound was lethal."

If Byron hadn't been a coward, he'd be alive, and this hatred between two families that had once been friends wouldn't exist. Actually, if Simon and Byron had put their pride aside and had been willing to discuss the matter, all this pain and turmoil could've been avoided.

Another bird soared overhead, and Eden squinted up, marking its path. She rubbed her forehead with her fingertips before sliding her thoughtful regard to the clearing once more.

"So, Simon never intended to kill your brother?"

"I don't believe he did, but my father didn't see it that way. He refused to consider that Byron's own spinelessness cost him his life. Father was overwrought with grief, unable to think rationally. I believe for his sanity's sake, he had to find someone—something—to blame. Father simply couldn't accept the truth." Still couldn't, and the inability had warped his reason. "That Byron had been a poltroon. Such a black mark against the duchy couldn't be tolerated or acknowledged. Honor above all else and all that rot, you know."

His diligence slipped and cynicism weighted his last words, making them more strident than he'd intended.

"And now Simon and his grace are so filled with hatred, logic escapes them," she said.

A bump in the road sent her hair to swaying. The

long strands, hanging past her waist, brushed the curve of her nicely rounded bottom bouncing on the seat.

Chester wasn't sure which tempted him more—her swaying hair or her pert bum.

He was determined to move on, forge a new reputation for the duchy, and perhaps in time, reconciliation between the Andrews and the DeCourcys might occur. Surely his running into Eden was fate. Well, to be precise, she'd run into him. But the point was, they seemed to be getting on famously.

It was a start at mending the breach between their families.

He hoped it would become much more.

He couldn't recall the last time he'd talked so comfortably with a woman, was so at ease in her presence. He didn't have to worry she'd misconstrue an innocent remark in the hopes of snaring herself a dukedom. He didn't have to feign interest in bobbles and gewgaws nor endure inane conversations about the weather and what the latest *on dit* circling the upper parlors was.

"Eden, may I ask you something personal?"

"You may, my lord, but I cannot promise to answer."

Blunt as always. Was she even capable of dissembling?

She hadn't chastised him for using her given name and not the more proper Miss Eden. That was a good indication, wasn't it? Yet, she insisted on using his title. Not that he blamed her. Those not born into nobility had decorum drilled into them from birth, always to respect the peerage. Nonetheless, he'd far prefer Eden thought of him as a man and not an aristocrat.

"Why do you defy fashion and wear your hair down? I'll admit I quite like it." He did. Even now, he itched to run his fingers through the shiny strands to see if they were as luxurious as they appeared. "Your hair is lovely, such an unusual shade." Light honey. That was the color. Rich and sleek. "But most women do their utmost to conform to society's strictures."

Then again, Eden certainly wasn't like other women. Most assuredly wasn't anything like the *haut ton's* elites, which was exactly why he found her so deuced alluring.

She gazed at him for another of those long, contemplative moments. So long, he found himself drowning in the pools that were her eyes. At last, she gathered her hair into a long, thick rope and lifted it off her neck. Angling her head, she exposed her nape.

"I have an unsightly birthmark that draws unpleasant attention if I wear my hair up."

5

Chester lifted a finger to graze the smooth brownish-red discoloration but caught himself and instead gripped the back of the seat.

The wine-colored spot covered most of Eden's nape and extended both into her cloak's collar and into her hairline.

He could well imagine her chagrin if others hadn't been kind about the irregularity.

"I don't think it's unsightly."

True, the blemish wasn't something overlooked upon first seeing it, but neither did the birthmark compel him to gawk.

After releasing her hair, she picked up the ribbons

once more and hitched a shoulder. Her nonchalance about the matter was a learned skill, he'd be bound.

"You are a kind man, and I think perhaps you try to find the good in others and in situations. Unfortunately, people of your character are scarce."

Her compliment chaffed his conscience. Eden had only seen the charming, roguish Manchester Sterling, not the man he kept well restrained.

As a pair of birds whisked over their heads, she pressed her lips into a rueful closed-mouth smile. Raising up on the seat, she watched the birds' meandering progress.

"The redwings will be migrating back to Scandinavia soon. I'm surprised they haven't already. They're very late in doing so this year. I like to sit outdoors at night and listen to them."

She'd artfully changed the subject.

So be it.

Chester didn't want her to be uncomfortable. He squinted at the birds as they swooped onto a Wentworth elm branch. His lack of knowledge regarding avian behavior of any sort chagrined him.

He'd never before cared what flitted overhead or amongst the bushes and trees.

Did that make him a self-centered sod like his sire?

The notion galled.

Fighting a yawn, he extended his legs, propped his elbows on the seat back, and after crossing his ankles, lifted his face to the sun. He'd missed the country's peacefulness and the invigorating freshness. Especially this time of year, with its abundance of foliage in bloom, filling the air with a heady natural perfume.

"At night?" he asked. "They're nocturnal? I had no idea."

He'd inquired about the birds simply to hear the low purr of her musical voice as she answered. Her speech lacked the affected air and often high-pitched simpering so many of the *ton's* damsels affected.

"Redwings migrate at night." She flinched again. The wagon seat wasn't comfortable and the jostling no doubt aggravated her bruised and battered body. "It's really quite spectacular to listen to. You ought to try it sometime, your lordship."

With her? Tonight?

A splendid notion. A midnight picnic, just the two of them. With champagne too.

Fine, mayhap tonight was a bit too soon, but assuredly next week was permissible.

A few peaceful minutes later, Eden guided the cart down a narrow, rutty lane, foot-high grass covering the center between the grooved tracks.

Chestnut feathered chickens dozed in the sun or pecked the ground for insects on one side of the pathway just wide enough for the cart to pass through, and a small, well-tended orchard lay beyond the poultry yard. A half dozen woven conical bee skeps rested on low platforms amongst the fruit trees.

An aged man limped near what must be the barn—if the sagging excuse for a building could be called that. Upon spying Eden, the elderly chap raised a hand in greeting, and Eden gave a cheery wave in return.

"That's Old Ronald. He once worked at the big house but grew too old to tend the gardens by himself. He lives here now, doing what he can to help. He has a room in the back of the barn but takes his meals with us. I don't know what I'd do without him. He knows how to care for every type of plant, tree, and shrub."

What she didn't say was her brother had likely sacked Old Ronald when he became too decrepit to complete the work her miserly brother assigned him.

It wouldn't surprise Chester if she didn't take in every stray or needy creature around.

A decent sized greenhouse took up the rest of the yard, along with a flowerbed, three rows of rose bushes, and a vegetable patch. No small amount of work to be done at Briar Knoll, and Chester would be bound, given her slightly brown hands, Eden labored in the gardens herself.

On the lane's other side, a quaint white cottage glistened in the morning sun. Yellow window boxes overflowing with colorful blooms graced the two front windows on either side of the faded black arched door.

"I trust you are none the worse for your dip into the stream yesterday?"

Took him long enough to get around to that, hadn't it?

Stark fear seized him when she'd toppled into Black Beck, and the strong current dragged her farther and farther from him. Even now, the memory caused his heartbeat to quicken and his mouth to go dry.

"Except for a few bruises, I'm quite recovered." Face a shade paler, she gave a delicate shudder. "But until that bridge is repaired and has a rail added, I'm never crossing it again."

"I intend to speak to Father and our bailiff this very afternoon about the matter, and I've already sent men to block off the bridge so no other traveler meets the same fate."

Chester dropped his feet to the floorboard and smothered another yawn. Sleep had evaded him most of the night for numerous reasons, not the least of which was the remarkable woman perched beside him. Each time he closed his eyelids, her lively eyes and petal pink mouth invaded his musings.

She drove Peony to the ramshackle outbuilding, and Old Ronald shuffled from the barn.

"Here we are, your lordship. Briar Knoll Cottage."

As was her habit, probably because there weren't

often men about to offer their assistance, she jumped to the ground without waiting for Chester to help her.

He followed, then bent to scratch Mr. Wiggles's back.

The dog gazed at him adoringly for half a second before seeking his mistress with his trusting eyes.

"Miss Eden, I have a surprise for you." Old Ronald hobbled to the wagon, his lopsided smile matching his irregular gait. Not a hint of censure about her irregular homecoming, but rather fatherly affection warmed his kind, weathered face.

"You do?" Joy bloomed across her features, once again transforming her.

So, Miss Eglantina Haverden liked surprises, did she?

"What is it?" She drew back, suddenly wary, giving him a gimlet eye. "Please tell me, not another two-headed chick." She turned that acute regard on Chester. "They only lived six days. It was awful, poor things."

"No, nothing like that, miss. Look." He pointed an arthritic finger to a trio of sturdy rose bushes situated behind a hospitable wrought iron bench. "The roses have buds."

Eden tossed him an incredulous look as she hurried closer.

"Truly? It's the first time that I can recall, though Mama swears they bloomed years ago."

"My mother also grew roses." Chester ventured nearer as well. "What kind are they? I wonder if we've any at Perygrim?"

"I myself planted a start there many years ago, sir. Before . . ."

Old Ronald cleared his throat and dropped his gaze whilst hitching up his trousers.

"They are Blue Damask, a very rare rose, indeed," Eden offered in answer as she gingerly lifted a stem laden with five small buds. "I was prepared to give up on them this year and have the plants removed to make room for gooseberry bushes."

Probably so she could sell the fruit.

Old Ronald laughed and slapped his hip with one hand while tugging his raggedy brimmed straw hat lower on his head with the other. "Legend says the blooming of the Blue Damask rose is a good omen."

"I've never heard any such thing." The smile she bestowed upon the hunched servant held genuine affection. "What's this omen? We certainly could use a bit of luck."

She released the heavy stem and stretched her spine, then pressed a hand to her forehead and rubbed gently.

Had her headache worsened?

A tinge of pain lingered in her eyes. Weariness too.

Old Ronald's rheumy gaze grew serious, and his attention flitted to Chester then back to Eden. He pulled on his earlobe, his sudden unease palpable.

"Ronald? Aren't you going to tell us the omen?"

At last he muttered while toeing a pebble, "When the Blue Damask blooms, enemies become . . . lovers."

Chester's gaze locked with Eden's, and though the fat bees kept buzzing about, the birds continued to sing, and the chickens clucked and cackled, the world narrowed to a tiny prism where they gazed into the other's souls—at once discomfiting and exhilarating.

About that midnight picnic . . .

"Eden . . .?"

"Auntie Eg. Auntie Eg."

Two ruddy-cheeked boys, their hair a shade lighter than their aunt's, skipped from the barn.

Enveloping them in her embrace, she kissed the tops of their dark blond heads.

"Oh, my goodness. What are you doing here, my darlings? Did you sneak away from your tutor again? Your mama and papa will not be pleased. Though I am so happy to see you."

She kissed them each again.

Eglantina Eden Haverden liked children.

Chester did too.

He'd always hoped to find a wife who actually enjoyed bed sport and who wouldn't object to several offspring rather than the required heir and spare.

Ridiculously pleased at another similarity between them, he propped an elbow on the cart and enjoyed Eden doting on her nephews.

"We were looking at the chicks. I saw one hatch all by itself! Old Ronald said we might." This from the smaller chap with eyes the same lavender blue shade as his aunt's. He ran the sleeve covering his forearm across his drippy nose. A dirt smudge remained above his left brow.

The older fellow, a trifle more reticent than his exuberant brother, cocked his head. "He said we might have one of the chicks as our own? Is it true? Might we truly?"

Eden laughed, and Chester stood stalk still, spellbound by her sheer loveliness. None of this made any sense. His immediate and powerful attraction to someone who everyone from his father to *le beau monde* would deem unsuitable.

A misalliance if there ever were one.

Precisely what made Eden Haverden perfect. For him.

She was so wholly unexpected. Completely unique. A wisp of fresh air in a stale and fusty room.

"Yes, you may each pick one chick as your very own pet. You must name it too." She kissed each of their heads a final time.

"Eglantina! Explain yourself. What are you doing

in the company of this man?"

A shutter closed over the contours of Eden's delicate features as surely if she'd slammed stout wooden panels across a window as she faced Simon Andrews, protectively encircling her nephews with her slender arms.

Chester came 'round the dog cart, the urge to shield her from the furious man stalking toward them so overwhelming that he angled his body, intending to step in front of Eden and block Andrews's progress.

"Don't," she whispered, sliding Chester a sideways glance, her eyes all but pleading with him. "Don't say anything, I beg you. Let me handle this."

Chester indicated his acquiescence with the merest narrowing of his eyes and an infinitesimal nod.

She canted her head toward the cart. "Ronald, please tend to Peony."

"Yes, miss." Ronald grasped the horse's halter, but before leading her away, speared Andrews a reproachful look.

Hands on his hips, Andrews glowered at his sons. "How many times must I tell you not to address her as

Auntie Egg? She's Miss Eglantina to you." He made a shooing motion. "Go home. Now. And await me in the nursery. While you are there, consider what punishment is appropriate for defying me."

"Yes, Father," the eldest said, his repentant gaze cast to the ground.

Andrews speared Eden a reproachful glance. "I wonder how often this occurs behind my back?"

Her pretty mouth pinched before she again kissed the boys atop their heads. "Go along now. Do as your father says. You may visit the chicks later."

After sliding their aunt an apologetic glance, the boys lowered their towheads and, holding hands, marched up the path wending past the orchard like well-trained miniature soldiers.

Sweet little lads.

A wonder they were the product of Andrews's loins. Chester would've expected pointed teeth, clawed-fingered, snarling, horned demons.

"I am waiting, Eglantina! I said explain yourself."

Wrath rendering Andrews's contorted features almost comical, he folded his arms and regarded her with the same distaste as one would fresh cow manure on the dining table.

Eden raised her chin and met his angry glare straight on.

Bravo!

If Andrews had thought to subjugate her, he'd failed. Chester wanted to applaud her courage.

And plant Andrews a facer.

However, that was not the way to end this feud. Calmness and reason must triumph. He wasn't his father or late brother. They were the temperamental ones, given to spewing their ire with no thought or care about whom their foul tempers might harm or the lasting damage their outbursts might cause. He was the one who possessed calm reason as well as a long-suffering temperament.

No, he was the one who *displayed* cool reason. For the same wrath that tormented his sire and dead brother also rose up within him, but he'd learned to tame the beast. Usually.

But, damn his eyes; he so longed to cork the seething cur standing opposite.

Eden gathered her hair and pulled it over one shoulder to dangle across her chest.

Chester forbade his hungry gaze from resting on the same gentle slopes as the lucky curls.

"Lord Sterling's horse went lame in Newbury, Simon. Since we're his closest neighbors, I simply gave him a ride from The Fox and Falcon yesterday. And—"

"Where were you all of last night? Your mother was so frantic when you didn't return home, she sent word to the big house." Simon leveled a bitter scowl at the cottage. "Though that she thinks she can prevail upon me to assist her is beyond the pale. I was to have gone to town this morning. Which is why my sons thought they could sneak away to see you, I'll be bound."

There was the man Chester remembered. As arrogant as his father and resentful of being inconvenienced by a worried mother and begrudging his sons a visit with their aunt.

A beleaguered frown creased Eden's brow, and Chester didn't miss her balling the folds of her cloak in her hand or the pursing of her flawless mouth

"But a note was to be delivered, explaining that I'd fallen into the brook and was at Perygrim Park." She glanced up at Chester, something close to accusation darkening her regard.

"Did the message not get sent?"

Curse it. Chester ought to have anticipated the duke's interference. Just the sort of thing his malevolent father would do.

He raised an apologetic brow and rubbed his chin. "I regret to say it's not impossible that my father may have had his man intercept the missive. I should've considered that possibility."

"Poor Mama. She must've been so distraught when I didn't come home." Eden swept her hair behind her as she flung an apprehensive glance toward the cottage. "I must reassure her all is well."

Andrew's face flushed a ruddy shade, somewhere between radish and cod. Not becoming in the least, especially considering the foppish raspberry colored suit he wore. He rather resembled an oversized, cooked lobster.

"Do you mean to say, you spent the night at Perygrim unchaperoned? With this man in residence? Have you taken complete leave of your senses? Of your scruples, Eglantina?"

6

Accustomed to Simon's long-winded rants, Eden nevertheless clamped her teeth and fisted her hands. She would not lose her temper in front of his lordship.

"I was chaperoned the entire time. A maid stayed in my chamber, and I didn't even venture below to eat, but instead had a tray brought to my chamber."

"A maid? A *maid*?" Simon scoffed. "Who will believe such a farce? Servants can be bribed to say anything."

Clearly, he preferred to think the worst of her.

"Now, see here. I daresay you've completely misunderstood the situation."

Lord Sterling stepped forward, his expression so outraged, she truly believed he might attempt to throttle Simon. His hunter green cutaway edged in black velvet made his eyes appear almost bottle green in his anger.

"You'd do well to tend to your own business, Sterling."

"I've made Miss Eden my business."

Such command of presence and such vehemence accompanied his declaration, Eden blinked in astonishment.

Simon's eyebrows vaulted skyward at that assertion, but before he could object, Lord Sterling said, "Your sister was soaked and freezing from having fallen into Black Beth last evening when the bridge gave way. I feared she'd catch lung fever."

"It's true, Simon. I almost drowned, and his lordship saved me."

Her brother's scathing look suggested he'd have preferred that she perished.

It had always been so, no matter how hard she tried to befriend him.

Lord Sterling scratched his head, his severe regard raking over Simon. "Would you have her sent home wet and bedraggled in the midst of last night's storm? Risk her health or take a chance of another mishap along the way?"

"Yes, if it meant preserving her reputation and not staining mine in the process." Simon snarled—actually snarled—and Mr. Wiggles whimpered, cowering closer to Eden's feet.

No surprise there; Simon always thought of himself first.

"Be reasonable, Simon—"

He cut her off with a curt, dismissive gesture. "I don't want to hear your contrived excuses. They matter naught." He stabbed a finger toward Eden. "You've been compromised. You should've thought of the consequence before climbing into a bed at Perygrim. You're of the same ilk as your drab of a mother. A lowborn trollop."

Eden recoiled as if slapped. But only for a flash, before she jutted her pert chin out and glared at him.

"How dare you?" she said, barely able to cobble

together a rational response through the red-hot haze of wrath engulfing her.

The spring sun might've burned away the morning's chill, but the hatred emanating from him sent an icy shiver scuttling down her spine. His objection had less to do with her poor choice to stay at Perygrim and much more to do with his hostility because she even existed.

Brother or not, if she were a man, she'd call him out.

Head elevated in his customary haughty fashion, one leg cocked and a hand on his hip, he taunted, "Best watch yourself, Sterling, lest she try to entrap you as her conniving mother did my father."

Eden's breath caught on a gasp, and Mr. Wiggles pushed against her ankles in concern.

"That's a foul lie, as you know full well. You despicable knave!"

A brusque sound of contempt rattled in his lordship's throat, and he went rigid, his posture menacing.

"You overstep the mark, Andrews. Have a care,

for I shan't permit you to insult Miss Eden again without consequence."

She abhorred violence, but she was feminine enough to appreciate a man defending her honor. For the very first time in her life, a male championed her. The foreign sensation bumping around her chest was secondary to the pulse raging at the base of her throat, however.

So much for the past years mellowing anyone's tempers.

Having reached the end of her endurance, she strode to her half-brother. Petite like her mother, hands propped on her hips, she glowered up at him.

"Simon, you may say whatever you like about me, for I don't give a snap for your opinion. But you will not defame my mother. Neither do I care if you believe me. Just because you do not doesn't mean that I'm deceitful."

Though he towered above her, she pulled herself to her full height and poked his chest.

He looked so startled and offended, she poked him again, just for good measure. Then, voice lowered and trembling with outrage, she delivered the *coup de grâce*.

"Lest you need reminding, Mama didn't come willingly to your father's bed, and though he later dismissed all the servants who knew the truth, the proof was irrefutable. He should've had charges brought against him, and one can only speculate why he did not." She swept her hand toward the humble cottage. "That's why we live here and why you pay us a pitifully small monthly stipend."

Familiar mortification washed over Eden, but she refused to be cowed or hang her head in shame. The truth was the truth, no matter how sordid or distasteful. Although she'd far prefer Lord Sterling hadn't learned the ugly details.

She'd been nauseated for a week upon accidentally discovering those unsavory particulars in Mama's forgotten journal eight years ago. Even the documents drawn up by Mama's brother, a solicitor, contained several incriminating lines. Uncle Frederick had died five years ago, and there was no one else to substantiate the claim now.

Thrice in the last year Briar Knoll had been searched whilst they were at church. Fearing Simon would find and destroy the agreement—the only thing forcing him to comply with the arrangement Walter Andrews had made with Mama—Eden had hidden the document away. That, in addition to his wife Candace's constant complaints regarding the monies paid to Eden, made her suspect Simon had suffered a reverse in fortune of some sort.

As much as Eden loathed accepting a shilling from Simon, her mother was entitled to the compensation and far more for what she'd endured. Maybe someday women would have recourse in similar situations, but current laws favored men. Eden knew full well Mama was fortunate to have any agreement at all. That she did revealed just how greatly Walter Andrews had wronged her and feared his actions exposed.

"You recklessly tossed propriety aside and stayed the night at a man's house, Eglantina."

Simon's harsh accusation brought her crashing back to the present.

She'd inadvertently provided him the excuse he'd

been seeking to put her out, she realized with a start. Not only had she acted impulsively, she'd disregarded the clause in the agreement that stipulated she and Mama must not do anything that drew attention or notice.

Simon even objected to them attending Sunday services. If he had his way, they'd never leave Briar Knoll Cottage.

"You've brought this upon yourself. I cannot have my sons associating with a woman of questionable virtue. You are forbidden to see them anymore."

His words, sharp as thorns, elicited a wince and lanced straight to her heart.

Not his name-calling.

Simon and Candace had said worse to Eden over the years. But to deprive her of Timothy and Prentice's precious company was truly painful to accept. The only affection the darlings received came from Eden and Mama. How could Simon punish his son's just to spite Eden?

The curtains shifted, revealing her mother's pale, anxious face in the window.

The raised voices had alerted her, no doubt.

Each time Simon called, Mama experienced a setback that put her in bed for a week. Her frail constitution and weak heart couldn't withstand any more shocks.

Squaring her shoulders, Eden notched her chin higher yet.

"I have done nothing wrong, Simon, and my conscious is clear. Now I must ask you to leave. You're upsetting Mama." She almost dared to say her nephews were welcome anytime, but feared he'd take a strap to them. "It would be best if you refrained from coming here in the future. Should you need to speak to me, send a missive and I shall come to Gablecrest."

Silence and a calculating look greeted her request.

A hen squawked, followed by a rooster's crow. Yet her brother remained silent, an enigmatic expression pulling the corners of his mouth downward. If he weren't such a petulant pout all the time, he'd be a handsome man.

"You heard her, Andrews. Be on your way, and unless you wish to earn more of my ill-favor, leave her and her mother alone."

Eden couldn't prevent the grateful glance she sent his lordship or the miniscule upward tip of her mouth. It was rather wonderful to have someone speak on her behalf for a change. She'd been the advocate for the household since returning home from school, and truth to tell, few people listened to her, a woman with no champion, let alone supported her.

Simon and Candace least of all.

"I remind you, Sterling, you have no say regarding either of them. Why are you even here?"

"None of your business."

Simon straightened his gaudy waistcoat, then fussed with his jacket lapel.

"But I do wonder what transpired betwixt the two of you that you presume such boldness and familiarity on such a short acquaintance?" Simon said while assuring his neckcloth was yet stiff enough to hold a fully ripe pumpkin.

Only a bufflehead could mistake his blatant innuendo.

"I'm warning you for the last time. Just one more

word, and I shall forget that I'm a gentleman and that when I returned home, I did so determined to end the squabble between our families." Lord Sterling advanced, ire radiating off him in scorching waves.

Was this typical behavior, or had Simon provoked this wrath?

Lord Sterling flexed his hand, a hard smile playing around the edges of his firm mouth. "I think I'd rather enjoy rearranging your face."

"You could try." An equally uncompromising glint shone in Simon's eyes.

Eden put a staying hand on Lord Sterling's arm. "My lord. Don't."

In truth, the men were well-matched in size and weight.

Simon and his lordship must not come to blows, for undoubtedly a duel would follow. Timothy and Prentice needed their father, even if he was an intolerable man, and his grace needed his son too. Despite Lord Sterling and the duke refusing to acknowledge that truth.

"Simon is goading you. It's what he does. He

enjoys poking and harassing until he gets a reaction, and then acts like he's the victim."

How many times had Eden seen him take this tactic? Most often with her. Unfortunately, more often than not, she eventually lost her patience and reacted, just as he'd hoped she would.

"And you'll what, Sterling? Call me out?"

Simon's derisive laugh rang harshly in the peaceful surroundings.

"Do you think I'm afraid? You're as big a coward as your sniveling brother was. He pissed himself before the poltroon tried to flee the field. You just stood there, watching it all, and now you dare defend this tart?"

Haughty and full of self-importance, Simon pointed his aquiline nose in the air.

It did rather look like a bird's beak. A parrot's or a cockatoo's in particular.

"You may hold a title, Sterling, but neither you nor your kin know a modicum about gentlemanly honor or pride."

Before Eden could blink, Simon lay upon his

back, blood trickling from the corner of his mouth. He spat into the dirt as Mama, leaning on Mattie's arm, shuffled from the house.

"Eglantina? What goes on here?" Mama called. "Why did that young man strike Simon?"

Bother and rot.

Eden didn't dare let her regard stray from Simon's infuriated countenance. She made a shooing motion behind her.

"Mama, go back into the house, please. Mattie, take her inside and make her tea. I'll be in shortly and explain."

To her knowledge, Simon had never been humiliated like this before, and God only knew how he might respond. His puffed-up pride knew no end, and he put tremendous import on appearances. Plus, he truly did think himself superior, and Lord Sterling had neatly knocked him down a peg.

From the corner of her eye, she covertly scanned the area for a weapon. A garden hoe or a shovel would do. Even a fist-sized rock would suffice, should he be rash enough to attack his lordship.

A flash of heat engulfed her, and she swallowed against the prickly sensations tickling her throat.

Could she actually strike Simon? Her own brother?

By jingle, to defend his lordship she could.

That revelation would have to be dissected later when she could ponder exactly why.

Besides, Simon had never acted the least bit brotherly toward her. Ever.

"I demand satisfaction." Simon could barely get the words past his clenched jaw.

Of course he did, dash it to ribbons.

Simon spat again whilst sitting up, and after wiping the blood away with his handkerchief, brushed the dirt from his over-bright trousers and coat.

"Name your second, Sterling."

"No. There will be no duel, Andrews. You insulted a lady and got what you deserved for your insolence. And to think I was going to persuade Father to invite you and your wife to the house party he's having. More fool I."

Lord Sterling, a muscle ticking in his jaw, paced

away as if he didn't trust himself to remain near Simon. His long legs, encased in biscuit-colored pantaloons, ate up the ground as he stalked toward the conservatory. Shoulders rising and falling in his agitation, he raked a hand through his mahogany colored hair. Several ruffled strands remained poking upright in what might've been an endearing fashion if the situation weren't so volatile.

A rush of relief so strong swept Eden that she closed her eyes and pulled in a long gulp of air. At least Lord Sterling had kept his head as far as a duel went. She'd never forgive herself if he, too, were shot because he felt the need to defend her honor.

"Too cowardly to meet me, are you?" Derision accented every terse syllable Simon sneered.

Why wouldn't he let it go? Was he really so blood-thirsty? So reckless?

So blasted foolish?

He was addressing a peer of the realm, a future duke. Had he lost his senses entirely? The Andrews might be landed gentry, but Lord Sterling claimed generations of blueblood. The DeCourcys were powerful and influential. Commoners such as Simon, even wealthy landowners, ought to tread carefully before recklessly overstepping the bounds.

One glance at his tension-lined features revealed the answer.

Absolutely, he would.

Lord Sterling laughed, a cutting humorless explosion, as he swung around to face them.

"Not cowardice, Andrews. It's called common sense and reason. Both of which you'd do well to employ more frequently. Unlike you, I'm thinking of your two young sons who need their father. For make no mistake." He waved a careless finger toward Simon the way one waves an annoying fly away from a pastry. "You would not walk away from a match with me. I am not my brother, and you would not be the first or second or even the seventh man I've faced on a field of honor. I, however, have *always* finished unscathed."

Simon's bravado slipped, and his face assumed an ashen hue. He dabbed his sweaty, receding hairline with his bloodied handkerchief.

Eden's jaw sagged, and she blinked twice in disbelief.

Had Lord Sterling said seven?

He'd fought that many duels?

Over what?

She wasn't altogether certain she wanted to know.

Just what kind of man was he?

This angry, intimidating man with a temper easily triggered, or the charming, good-natured scamp she'd sat beside yesterday? Likely two sides of the same coin, for didn't everyone harbor a bit of darkness, even if they hid it well?

For certain she did.

A charged silence ensued, Simon and his lordship glaring daggers at each other. In the end, Simon averted his gaze first.

"I shall not countenance it, I tell you, Eglantina." Shaking his head, cruel satisfaction hardening the lines of his already lean face, Simon staggered to his feet. "You've brought disgrace upon me, my family, and our good name."

No, Simon, your father did that when he despoiled

my mother.

"Regardless of the embarrassment, I've endured you and your mother's presence for far longer than I should've out of respect for my father's wishes. I've paid the taxes on Briar Knoll and delivered your monthly allowances without complaint."

Hardly without complaint: always grudgingly and demeaningly. Making certain Eden and Mama knew how beholding they were.

"But no more." He stuffed his stained handkerchief in his pocket and slashed an unsympathetic glance to Mama, hovering with Mattie near the roses.

"I want you all gone from Briar Knoll within the week."

Mama, her face as white as the knitted shawl about her frail shoulders, let out a distressed cry and clutched at Mattie's arm.

"No."

Tears glistened in the servant's eyes as she tried to console Mama.

Eden gasped and wrenched her attention to his

gloating face.

"You've no right to evict us. There's an agreement—"

Simon smirked as he flicked a fleck of dirt off his elbow. "Have your solicitor contact mine. But we both know it will take months before the matter reaches the courts, and I'll make public your indiscretion. As landlord, I have the right to evict tenants without notice. I'm sure acting the part of a strumpet violates a portion of the contract."

"Of all the unconscionable, despicable blackguards." Lord Sterling swore beneath his breath, his face all harsh planes and angles.

"You know full well I cannot afford a solicitor, and we're not tenants." Simon might have her on the indiscretion bit though. She'd need to review the document.

Eden swallowed and shook her head to dispel the wave of dizziness and sudden heat battering her. Why had she ever agreed to stay at Perygrim? This entire fiasco would've been avoided had she not been impulsive and foolish. Not given in to a ridiculous whim to spend another few minutes with Lord Sterling.

A man far beyond her reach, and now she'd destroyed everything.

"One week, Eglantina." Simon cast a disinterested gaze about the yard. "Everything and everyone. Anything left behind I'll order burned."

She suspected this had been coming for some time, but the reality stole her breath. Casting a frantic glance around, she scoured her mind for a solution.

What would become of Mama? Old Ronald or Mattie? Acorn and Mr. Wiggles? The chickens? Her bees?

Where would they go? They had no one—*no one*—whom they could impose upon.

Her small savings wouldn't go far, and without the income from the produce and eggs, she'd never be able to take Mama to Bath for the waters now. That had been a desperate woman's dream.

Unable to stand the pity deepening Lord Sterling's eyes or the despair filling Mama's and Mattie's, Eden hugged her shoulders and, eyes brimming, chin tucked to her chest, whispered, "What will we do?"

"I truly care not." Simon gave a snide laugh and cut his lordship a challenging look. "Perhaps Sterling will accommodate you, since he seems so concerned with your well-being."

She commanded her clamoring thoughts and raging pulse to calm. Overwrought, she was of no use to anyone. Biting her pointer fingernail, she pursed her lips and sucked in a lengthy, steadying breath.

After Simon's pronouncement, he stomped up the path his sons had disappeared down minutes before.

No one said a word.

Even the chickens ceased cackling.

A moment later, Mama collapsed.

7

"I'll carry her inside. Quickly, prepare her bed," Chester instructed the middling-aged servant crouched over Eden's insensate mother.

Eden held her mother's hand and patted her pallid cheeks.

"Mattie, do as he asks, and get cold water from the well."

"Of course, Miss Eden." Mattie, swiping at her round, wet face with her apron, rushed to do Eden's bidding.

"Should I go for the physician, Miss?" Old Ronald hovered just outside the entrance to the barn, his face crumpled into deep grooves.

Mr. Wiggles walked in circles around Eden and her mother, whining low in his throat.

"No, not yet. She has medicine. She's just suffered a shock, I think." Eden brushed her mother's cheek with her bent index finger. "Mama, wake up."

"Allow me." Chester lifted the frail woman—she hardly weighed more than a sack of grain—then hurried into the humble cottage. Easy to see where Eden had acquired her petite form.

The instant they entered the cottage, a red squirrel scampered off a shelf and just as quickly darted up Eden's gown to sit atop her shoulder, chirping happily and fiddling with her hair.

"Not now, Acorn. Mama's not well. You'll have to wait to play. I'm sorry, sweet girl."

She kissed the squirrel's head, then placed the creature on the back of the divan where it sat on its haunches. Tiny black-nailed paws in the air and nose twitching, she nervously stared at Chester.

"This way, m'lord." Eden indicated a narrow, open door off the tidy main room beyond which Mattie plumped pillows for her mistress.

He nodded and wended his way through the tattered furnishings and across the nearly worn through rag rugs. Had she picked the flowers in the vase centered on the table? Perhaps knitted the throw dangling over the sagging armchair beside the unlit fireplace?

Humble, but homey. And filled with love. That was how the cottage struck him. He preferred it over Perygrim's cold, dispassionate grandeur.

After he settled Eden's mother atop the bed and Eden and Mattie rushed to make the now conscious but befuddled woman comfortable, Chester cleared his throat.

"May I speak with you outside, Miss Eden?"

The servant tossed him a curious glance as she crossed to a dressing table, its mirror foggy from age. Three cobalt blue medicine bottles stood side by side atop the table, along with a spoon, a pitcher, and a glass on a simple pewter tray.

Eden hesitated, but after sweeping a glance over her wan mother, gave a short nod. She kissed her mother's forehead, brushing her gray-threaded hair away from her thin face.

"I'll be right back. Don't do anything foolish while I'm gone." She winked and squeezed her mother's hand. "I don't want Mattie telling me you were attempting cartwheels or back flips again."

Miss Haverden offered a feeble smile and peered pointedly at Chester. "I believe an introduction is in order first, my dear."

"Oh, of course. Forgive me my poor manners."

The merest hint of color blossomed across Eden's cheeks as she removed her cloak, revealing her figure to him for the first time.

What she lacked in stature she made up for in lush form, for no one could doubt she was a woman fully grown and deliciously rounded in all the places that mattered: the places a man enjoyed curving his hands around. Her serviceable gown showed signs of repeated wear: frayed hem, worn elbows—and if he wasn't mistaken, a few skillful mends—and yet the unassuming garment didn't detract from her loveliness.

She bent over her mother again, straightening the coverlet. A team of draft horses couldn't have pried his appreciative gaze from the delightful view her upturned bottom provided. She straightened, and holding her mother's hand, indicated him.

"Mama, this is Manchester, Marquis of Sterling. My lord, my mother, Dulcina Haverden."

"The Duke's younger son?"

"I am." Chester inclined his head. "I am honored to make your acquaintance, and I pray you make a swift recovery."

A wadded handkerchief pressed to her mouth, the woman coughed, her thin shoulders quaking from the tremors.

Folding his arms, one elbow atop his forearm, Chester rested his chin on his fist. For certain he wasn't a physician, but he recognized illness when he saw it. What exactly was her ailment? Her prognosis? Was it as grim as his sire's?

Was that another thing he and Eden had in common? The looming loss of their remaining parent? But in her case, she adored her mother, while every jot of affection he'd ever held for Father had long since shriveled up and died.

Truly? Wasn't there an inkling of regard left for the duke?

Not any that he'd felt in a very long while.

That truth sobered him all the more.

Eden draped her wrap over the foot of the bed, her face creased with silent concern.

"Have a drink of water, Dulcina," Mattie said, extending a full glass.

After taking a sip, Miss Haverden passed it back. "I'm sure your father is delighted to have you home, my lord. Even when they've become adults, parents worry about their children."

The love-filled glance she gifted Eden with caused a twinge of envy behind Chester's breastbone.

Miss Haverden waved her blue-veined hand toward her daughter.

"Go on, Eglantina. I'm perfectly fine."

Smoothing another quilt over her mother's lap, Eden produced one of her famous infectious smiles, and despite the sobriety of the moment, Chester's lips twitched in answer.

"I'll be back in a few minutes, Mama. I'll bring

tea too, and Jane sent hot cross buns for you."

How Eden could command such poise when her brother had just turned her out and her mother had collapsed, Chester couldn't fathom, but he admired her even more for her valor.

Once in the sitting room, he examined the furnishings again. Everywhere he looked, he observed signs of stark poverty. A blanket covered the sagging settee's cushions, and except for two oval-framed dried flower arrangements, nothing decorated the stained and chipped walls. No gew-gaws cluttered the lone, sparsely filled bookshelf either.

Just then the squirrel, a small crust of bread in her mouth, zipped up his leg, over his torso, and onto his chest before becoming tangled in the folds of his neckcloth. The little beast's frantic cries weren't nearly as sharp as the claws trying to shred Chester's cravat, his neck, or his chin.

"Acorn. No."

Eden flew to Chester.

"Don't move, my lord. I'll untangle her. Can you tilt your chin up?"

And have the terrified vermin down his shirt in a trice?

God help him.

Obediently notching his chin toward the ceiling, he scrutinized the shabby roof that, if he wasn't mistaken, badly needed repair. Bare beams supported the sagging structure. He swore he could see daylight between the cracks in a few places.

The sweet essence of roses and irises floated upward from Eden's hair, and unable to resist, he glanced down.

"Acorn, hold still. You're going to scratch his lordship."

Too late.

Lower lip pinched between her white teeth, she worked to free her panicked pet. More than once her fingers brushed his neck and chin, and though the touch wasn't in the least meant to be seductive, his body responded like a stag in rut.

A dip in the chilly lake was in order. As soon as possible.

"There we are." Holding Acorn tucked below her

chin, Eden met his eyes, her expression adorably contrite. "I beg your . . ."

Her gaze dropped to his mouth and lingered.

What would she do if he kissed her?

Right here? Right now?

For nearly twenty-four hours he'd imagined doing so. Ever since her mouth parted in surprise at the Fox and Falcon.

He dipped his head until a mere two inches separated their mouths.

She hauled her gaze to his.

He wasn't able to conceal his scorching desire swiftly enough, and she retreated a step.

Too much too soon.

"Pardon. I beg your pardon, my lord." she said, her voice breathy even as she dared another peek at his mouth. "Acorn quite ruined your cravat, I fear."

The squirrel scooted farther into her hair, scolding Chester all the while.

Impudent little vermin. Admonishing him when she'd mistaken him for a tree.

Touching his neck, he tried to determine just how

many scratches he'd sustained. Something slid down his shirt, landing where the fine lawn was tucked into his trousers. The bread no doubt. Likely why Acorn continued to fuss and fret.

"You wanted to speak with me?" Eden raised one side of a sewing table and set Acorn within. "She's made herself a nest inside," she offered by way of explanation.

He cut a speculative glance toward her mother's room. "I must return to Perygrim to meet with my father's physician and the bailiff. Please allow me to have the doctor look in on your mother too. At my expense."

"That's very gracious of you, but Dr. Munson visited last week and prescribed new medication. I couldn't possibly permit you to pay in any event. It wouldn't be proper."

She straightened a limp needlepoint pillow, the stitching missing in several places and the corners looking to have been nibbled.

The squirrel again? Or other vermin?

"I understand," he said. "Perhaps later in the week

if she hasn't improved?"

Her mother's rasping breaths carried into the small entry.

Just how ill was Dulcina Haverden?

"I don't know where we'll be in a week." Despair drove the light from Eden's eyes.

He had a thought about that. A solution, perhaps. If she were agreeable.

Not entirely respectable, but there were far worse propositions.

"Oh, I almost forgot. Wait here. I'll be right back." She disappeared through a doorway to what must be the kitchen. A few moments later, she reappeared carrying a small jar of umber colored honey. She handed it to him. "I know I'm a day late, but birthday felicitations to you."

Such a simple gesture, but something welled in his chest, making speech impossible for a moment. It had been a very long while since he'd received a gift. A very long while, indeed. This jar of glistening honey mightn't be the most elaborate or costly he'd been given, but it was the most meaningful, because she'd given it out of the goodness and generosity of her heart.

She, who had so little, and was about to lose her home, had thought to remember his birthday. Because she was kind and good and thoughtful.

"Thank you, Eden."

"You're welcome."

Neither did she apologize for the simplicity or humbleness of the gift, and he was glad. That would've diminished its specialness.

She'd crossed to stand before one of the windows. Her profile and drooping shoulders revealed the great weight she carried.

Silence fell between them, not uncomfortable, but filled with questions neither dared to ask.

"Eden?"

"You really shouldn't address me by my given name, my lord. Miss Eden isn't all that proper, but two Miss Haverdens proved much too confusing. I also wanted to try to lessen my mother's humiliation."

"I shouldn't, I vow, but I like saying your name. I promise to only do so when no one can overhear us. Is that acceptable?" The smile he slashed her wasn't the least repentant.

"I suspect you'll do what you like no matter what I might say. I've generally found it to be so." She glanced toward her mother's room. The slightest jot of acrimony tinged her words.

Life had taught her that bitter truth, and it didn't sit well with him that he should be lumped with other nobles and gentry.

"I should check on Mama."

"I have another matter I'd like to discuss with you. Outside, please."

Eden gazed at him expectantly as they crossed to the door. "Yes? Can you give me a hint?" Sudden wariness slowed her steps. "It's not more bad news is it?"

"No, nothing of that nature." He opened the door and stood aside for her to pass. "Perygrim is in need of a housekeeper, and our gardens are not what they once were. I thought perhaps . . . What I mean is, given the regrettable turn of events . . . That is perhaps . . ."

Could he be any more fumbling or inept?

An uncertain expression, part hope and part skepticism skated across her features. She grabbed his arm and all but hauled him over the threshold with her. After closing the door behind them, she ventured in a quiet voice, "Are you offering Mattie and Old Ronald employment?"

He'd actually thought Eden might consider the housekeeper position herself, but given her immediate assumption he'd meant Mattie to fill the position, she likely would've been insulted at the suggestion.

Make her your mistress

That devilish part he kept well-subdued dared to whisper the provocative notion.

He soundly kicked the taunt to the stable manure pile where that kind of filth belonged.

Diligence and discipline, old chap.

Tucking the small jar of honey into his jacket pocket, he nodded. "I am, if you—"

"Oh, thank you. Thank you."

Her grateful smile didn't quite reach her sad eyes, now a shade closer to eggshell rather than the palest periwinkle blue they were when she was happy.

What color would they be filled with passion? Sapphire?

"I didn't know what was to become of them, for I cannot hire a solicitor to fight Simon in court. And I simply do not have the means to feed two more people."

He'd venture to guess, she didn't even have the resources to feed herself or her mother.

"With your permission, I could retain a solicitor for you."

Eden shook her head, her curtain of hair swirling around her shoulders and back as she made her way to the chicken pen.

He yearned to run his fingers through the thick mane. To gather her in his arms and assure her that she needn't worry or fret over her future. But he had no business making any such promise on such short acquaintance. Any promises at all, truth to tell.

By the time he caught up to her, she'd tossed a few handfuls of cracked corn to the excited chickens, rushing here and there, pecking the grain and occasionally each other in their rush to gobble the most food. Brushing her hands together to rid them of the grain dust, she regarded him for a discomfiting moment, as if considering his offer.

Then with a slow sweep of her dark lashes across her sun-kissed cheeks, she shook her head again.

"Thank you, but I cannot accept. For even if I should prevail in court, my lord, I could never repay you. And though my station is humiliating, and it may seem ridiculous to you, I do retain a degree of pride. I've kept us out of debt this long, and I shan't venture down that path now."

He wasn't surprised she'd refused. Eden's pride wasn't puffed up arrogance, conceit, or misplaced self-importance, as was often the case. Hers was more about dignity and self-respect, which showed in her strength of character and lack of self-pity.

"What will you do then?"

Her further reduction in circumstances abraded his composure. The unfairness chafed his sense of justice, and the dark temperament he'd meticulously kept under control, except for fleeting interludes, pulsed in his veins, demanding vengeance.

Another idea sprang to mind, but the inkling was so outside the bounds, Chester wanted to ponder it a bit more. Consider the feasibility. The ramifications for her as well.

"I have a few options."

She stared into the orchard while toying with a dull, silverish button at her throat. Emotions played across her gentle features as she silently pondered her circumstances.

"I haven't enough education, nor do I play any instruments or speak French, and my singing induces loyal Mr. Wiggles to howl. So that eliminates the possibility of becoming a governess. I might find employment as a companion if it weren't for the need to care for Mama. Perhaps Jane Stewart will hire me to wait tables or clean, even cook. I don't mind hard work."

Not likely. Even as goodhearted as they were, the Stewarts couldn't afford to pay her the wages she'd need to provide for her mother.

"What about your mother?"

"If I let a room at the Fox and Falcon, I could

check in on Mama throughout the day."

He wasn't going to crush her hope. She'd little else to cling to.

"Have you any other possibilities?"

It wasn't any of his business, but he couldn't abandon her. More on point, he doubted she had anyone to talk to, to share her worries and concerns with.

She closed her eyes and swallowed before putting a delicate hand to her throat.

"I . . . Vicar Wright has proposed marriage more than once. He assures me Mama is welcome too."

Something akin to a stone-laden wagon smashed into Chester's middle.

Marriage?

Why hadn't he considered that?

Eden was an attractive, desirable woman, and from what he'd learned about her in their short acquaintance, spirited but considerate as well.

"Do you love him?"

Way beyond the mark asking such a personal question.

She wet her lower lip, darting her pink tongue out and tracing it across the plump pillow.

Ferocious lust gripped him, and he imagined sinking his mouth onto her sweet, moist lips.

Had she ever been kissed?

Had the Vicar ever dared taste those dewy lips?

He would, and much more, if Eden wed him.

Again, a sensation akin to a plow horse's kick to Chester's gut cramped his middle. That ugly blackness welled up inside, but he doggedly squelched the feeling. He had no claim on Eden Haverden.

Flattening the line of her mouth, she shook her head and sighed.

"I wish I could. He's kind and decent. Generous and gentle and quite handsome too."

A proverbial saint, blast the honorable cleric.

"But you don't?"

An inkling of hope rekindled.

"I do not. I've tried to, believe me. He'd make a wonderful husband, and I'm quite fond of his daughters."

She'd be a wonderful mother.

She wandered to the bench situated before the roses. Sinking onto the white paint-chipped seat, she looked overhead, her expression contemplative. Mr. Wiggles trotted to her and laid his scruffy head on her knees. She absently petted him whilst gazing at the sky.

"I fear the parish would object. Because of my birth."

She probably had that right. Even commoners oft' frowned upon those born out of wedlock, though why anyone thought it appropriate to blame the progeny baffled him. Of course, if she had a rich father—well she had, but he'd not bestowed a dowry upon her—she might've married well. Blueblood by-blows often made good matches. Or she might've chosen to remain independent, had Walter Andrews bequeathed a yearly allowance on her.

Yes, but Eden Haverden wasn't aristocracy. She had no dowry or one hundred pounds a year. Her choices were neither plentiful nor pleasant.

Chester sank onto the wobbly bench, and because her small hand was within reach, he covered it with his palm. But only for instant. That was enough time for another jolt to sluice through him and another notion, this much more wicked than his prior one to leap to the forefront of his mind again.

She'd make a splendid mistress

He could set her up in her own house. Arrange for someone to care for her mother. Hell, even let her have her chickens and bees and that terror of a squirrel too.

Where had his control, vigilance, his discipline scampered off to?

Even his carnal urges and randy thoughts were refusing to bend to his will.

More on point, where had his decency and chivalry got to?

In his very bones he knew Eglantina Eden Haverden would never agree to be a kept woman. She'd hate herself, and at the moment, he didn't regard himself with any great fondness for even minutely entertaining such a degrading thought about her.

"And you've no other family or friends?"

She'd said she didn't, but he wanted to be sure before he made his proposition.

"None. Simon's sisters have always been much kinder than he, but neither has ever showed any interest in a relationship with me. Mama's brother died five years ago."

"So, you truly have no alternatives?"

She pursed her lips and assumed a thoughtful mien. "There's always a soiled dove or mistress, though I'm not entirely sure how one goes about either."

A moment ago, he'd very briefly entertained the same notion, and now coming from her sweet mouth, the suggestion sounded as vile as any he'd ever heard.

Eden would never stoop so low.

Not as long as *he* drew breath.

She crossed her ankles and flicked that blue-eyed gaze over him.

In reproach?

"You needn't look so affronted. I'm but teasing, my lord. My, but you do blow prickly one minute and jovial the next. It's a bit disconcerting."

Years of carefully constructed walls and embedded behaviors, brought about by deliberate intent, crumbled with her observation.

"Eden, I would never let you be reduced to such desperate circumstances."

"I appreciate the noble sentiment, but we both know I'm not your responsibility." She winced slightly, then coughed into her hand. "I beg your pardon."

Her voice held the merest bit of scratchiness. Was she becoming ill? On top of the other blows she'd been dealt today?

Chester slapped his knees.

By God he'd do it. Toss common sense and decorum to the four corners of the earth.

Father very well might suffer an apoplexy.

People would no doubt twitter and gossip.

His friends, particularly the Duke of Harcourt and Alex Wimpleton, would claim he'd lost all reason, but if Eden was amendable to the suggestion, what did it matter?

If his father wanted him to consider settling down, he must compromise as well. This would be the first battle. Maybe not the first. Last night's skirmish fit that description. For what Chester was about to propose, he might need full body armor when he next faced his sire.

He took her hand again, turning it over so her palm faced upward. She had a small, healing blister on the middle finger of her right hand.

She didn't object, just regarded him curiously.

"Eden, I have need of a secretary. The position is yours if you want it. You'd have a suite of rooms at Perygrim and a house or apartment in London. Your mother may, of course, live with you, as well as a nurse to help care for her."

Eden regarded him as if he'd sprouted another head. A very grotesque head.

"My lord, forgive my frankness, but I do not know of a single female secretary. What you're suggesting is scandalous. It's impossible."

"Well, it's time that was changed. Females are every bit as capable as males, and you've proven you have a good head for business. Why, someday I suspect you'll see women doing many of the things only men are permitted to do. You can read and write and, I assume, calculate sums. What do you say? At least consider it."

A slow smile bent her bowed lips. "Very well. I'll consider it, but later. I've had a trying last four and twenty hours, and in truth, I'm feeling a bit done in."

At least she hadn't refused outright.

"Fine. I'll call in a day or two and you can give me your answer." Was tomorrow too soon? "I can also arrange to have Perygrim's staff assist you with your move."

"That's very generous of you." A mischievous twinkle appeared in her eyes. "I don't suppose you have any need for a flock of chickens or bee hives?"

Crossing his ankle over his knee, Chester laid his arm across the back of the bench. Eden's hair was right there; all he had to do was move his fingers an inch.

"I don't see why not. We've land enough for certain. And we haven't either chickens or bees."

"What about my pets? Acorn didn't make the best impression a bit ago. I'm quite sure her crust of bread is somewhere inside your shirt."

"They'll come with you, naturally." He patted his

waist, offering a wry grin. "As for her snack, it's right here.

She chuckled then, genuinely amused, and he couldn't prevent the upward tug of his lips.

"I cannot see his grace accepting a squirrel racing about the mansion. Acorn hides her treats everywhere. In the draperies, behind pillows and cushions, atop shelves. And she's not always discrete when she tends to her baser needs."

Ah, he hadn't considered that particular.

"I'm sure we can work something out. I did mention you'll have an entire suite of rooms to yourself, didn't I?" He put his finger to his chin. "Probably ought to give you access to the carriage, and I suppose a modest wardrobe befitting your position is also in order."

"I haven't accepted the position." She brushed at her gown before meeting his eyes. "You do realize how impetuous you're being? I wouldn't have taken you for the rash sort."

"I'm not, generally." Ever, really. Except with her. "But only this morning I became aware of the need for a new secretary." Best see to giving Dockery his *congé* at once. "And it was pure happenstance that I was here when your brother put you out."

Rubbing Mr. Wiggles's head, she gave him a tired half-smile. "What if I decline, which is the practical and proper thing to do?"

Chester stood. He really needed to be off. If he cut through the oak copse and skirted the lake, he could be home in half an hour.

"Well then, my dear Miss Eglantina Eden Haverden, I shall make the offer so appealing you simply cannot refuse. I shall brook no refusal."

8

Three evenings later, Eden sat in a rocking chair outside the cottage entrance. Eyes shut and hands folded in her lap, she sighed and slowly tipped the chair back and forth. The rhythm had always calmed her. Mama said it was so even when she'd been an infant.

Weary to her marrow, she slowly opened her eyes.

A cough rattled in her chest, and she covered her mouth with her handkerchief lest Mama hear.

She'd not felt well since her tumble into the stream, and today, she'd been alarmed to realize she burned with fever. There was no time to be sick. No funds to hire a doctor either.

The black pepper and honey tea she'd been drinking seemed to help a bit, as did the thyme tea she'd brewed.

Three days of sorting and packing, only taking what was essential had proved more difficult than she'd imagined. Daily trips to Newberry seeking employment had proved futile and a sense of panic assailed her, knotting her stomach and keeping her awake at night.

Jane had tearfully explained she couldn't afford to hire Eden, but she'd offered to let her and Mama a small chamber for a fraction of what they generally charged. Even so, there was food to buy and Mama's medicine, and without a source of income, Eden would soon run through her small savings. Jane wouldn't permit pets either.

If Eden had to give up her beloved Mr. Wiggles and Acorn too, she very well might fracture.

Each business she'd approached had given her the same answer. She offered no real skills or talents, and their pitying smiles or averted glances shredded her remaining pride. On the trek home yesterday, she'd burst into tears and cried, great gasping, heartbroken sobs into Peony's sturdy warm, wonderfully horsey-smelling neck.

Eden couldn't remember the last time she'd cried like that.

Yes, she could.

When she'd been sent off to boarding school.

The same helplessness enshrouded her now.

She put a hand to her forehead where a headache had nagged for days.

She stopped rocking.

Lord Sterling had not put in his promised appearance.

She told herself to stop listening for a carriage or horse, to cease glancing out the window a hundred times a day. And yet, a tiny ridiculous hope remained that he'd come.

Her unlikely knight to the rescue.

She shouldn't feel this intense disappointment.

He'd made the impractical, gallant offer out of pity. Once home, he'd no doubt realized the impossibility of retaining her as his secretary.

Hopefully he planned to hire Mattie and Old Ronald. And to move the chickens and bees to Perygrim. She also meant to ask him if he would consider taking Peony. She wasn't a beautiful high stepper, but she was sweet and gentle.

A flush of embarrassment infused her. She'd imposed upon him more than she had any right to, given their short association. Perchance that was the reason for his absence—she'd overstepped. Another wave of hot humiliation bathed her.

She had been reduced to beggary.

Just as Simon and Candace had accused her.

Eyes brimming once more, Eden scanned the peaceful horizon as she dashed away the moisture blurring her vision and coughed again.

This might be her last chance to appreciate the view she'd known since birth. As it did each day, the sun had bid the day *adieu* and the fiery orb would rise on the morrow as if nothing had changed.

Except she and her mother were a day closer to homelessness.

What would Simon do if they refused to leave?

Call the magistrate? Burn their belongings while they watched?

Neither was farfetched.

A full moon lit the heavens, so luminous it blanketed the earth in a silvery light.

The call of the redwings echoed across the night sky, a sound she once would've delighted in. Instead, she strained to hear if Mama had stopped weeping. Her mother had put on a brave front for Lord Sterling the other day, but when Eden had entered the cottage after his departure, she found her mother inconsolable.

Mama had been in that state since, crying herself to sleep every night.

For once, Eden couldn't dredge up assurances that they would be all right. She couldn't promise Mama anything.

Restless, tense, unresolved about what she was going to do, Eden rose. Across the way, Lake Blackton shimmered under the rising fairy moon. The cool air felt wonderful on her flushed face. No destination in mind, she wandered the path through the orchard, then continued on toward the lake. She rarely came this far anymore—hadn't in years—but this evening, something drew her onward.

It might've only been the desire to escape the melancholy that had settled on the cottage—a thick, stifling shroud of despair.

Such anger toward Simon roiled within, the hostility alarmed her. Made her loathe herself for the ugly thoughts invading her brain. She wanted to shout at the injustice. Throw dishes across the room. Slap his smug face. She could do none of those things, so she walked, swiftly and mindlessly to expend her frustrated energy and expel the demons taunting her.

Four more days.

That's all they had.

A decision must be made.

A decision *had* been made.

One born of utter hopelessness and despair.

A numbing calmness cloaked her, dispelling her anxiety and quieting her tumultuous musings. And also, effectively nullifying any foolish romantic notions she'd entertained.

As generous as Lord Sterling's offer of service

had been, to accept meant crossing several boundaries. Gossip and rumors would run rampant. Worse, though, would be residing in the same house as The Duke of DeCourcy.

Perhaps if his lordship had offered her use of The Lake House, she might've seriously considered his generous proposal despite the impropriety. But exposing Mama to the duke's enmity was inconceivable. She'd endured too much unhappiness already, and her remaining years should be spent in comfort. Not the target of a contemptible ill-tempered brute.

Besides, Mama couldn't live in London part of the year. She couldn't tolerate the sooty, polluted air, and leaving her at Perygrim—anywhere for that matter—was out of the question. You didn't abandon an ailing parent.

With no other viable options, practicality, combined with a great deal of desperation, had finally convinced Eden of what she must do.

"I can do it. I must," she muttered to herself as she strode the path.

Faithful as always, Mr. Wiggles trotted beside her.

A rueful smile bent her mouth.

At least with this solution, she wouldn't have to give up her pets along with everything else.

Tomorrow, she'd go into Newbury and accept Vicar Wright's proposal.

There was nothing else for it.

Throat tight, she swallowed and angrily dashed at the tears tracking over her cheeks. She'd be a good wife to Jedidiah. She would. She was frugal and kind. Patient most of the time. A decent cook, and she could sew a straight seam. She'd try to be a loving mother to his daughters, seven-year-old Emma and ten-year-old Dorothy.

As if her subconscious mind knew her ponderings all along, she found herself at the small lake's edge. The Lake Cottage, also painted white like Briar Knoll except it was considerably bigger, glowed bright in the moonlight. Bright because lights shone in the windows that had been dark for years.

Who was in residence?

A visitor?

Lord Sterling?

Where the lawn tapered downward, a dock extended into the lake, much like the landing on this side. There floated the small pier where she'd fallen into the lake and almost drowned.

She did remember, vividly, how terrified she'd been.

Eden picked up a handful of blackish stones, then as she walked the shoreline, tossed them into the water, watching until each ripple disappeared before throwing another in. She lifted her hand to send the last smooth rock sailing into the peaceful water, when a big splash drew her attention to the dock.

Had someone jumped off?

In a moment, a form bobbed to the surface and began lazily swimming on his back toward her.

She froze, curious and yet wary.

Who was it?

After a few minutes, he turned around and swam back to the dock, and she relaxed.

Until he climbed out, and she saw his naked bum. His very taut, very muscular naked bum, thighs, and back. And for the life of her, she couldn't look away.

She swallowed a sudden rush of . . . Whatever this feeling was heating her blood that prevented her from tearing her rapt gaze off his beautifully sculpted form. The Adonis grabbed a towel from a chair and wrapped the length about his waist before turning in her direction.

He gave a cocky wave.

"Eden, do you always lurk about the shore at night? Or were you spying on me?"

The next morning, Eden left the cottage before Mama awoke. She hadn't even taken the time to drink a cup of tea or eat a piece of toast.

Wearing her nicest frock, a jonquil and ivory empire-waisted morning gown, years out of fashion but quite lovely, she drove the dogcart down the deserted lane. She'd even donned her bonnet, its emerald ribbon tied in a jaunty bow to the left side of her chin, and wore her only pair of gloves. Her crocheted shawl lay on the seat where Mr. Wiggles usually sat.

She couldn't risk becoming covered in his hair. Her task was too important, and she must present herself as a lady. Perhaps not in the first tulip of fashion, but neat and poised. Respectable and modest. Qualities pastor's wives must master.

That peculiar tranquility that had overcome her last evening had abandoned her.

There'd been no remnant of calm composure as she'd dashed home, Lord Sterling's laughter pealing in her ears. She had not gone to the lake to spy on him, the conceited knave.

Even now, if she closed her eyes, she could see his magnificent form outlined in the moonlight. She'd unabashedly looked her fill too, until he recognized her.

More fool she, thinking he might've been called up to London and that's why he hadn't returned as he said he would. He'd been lazing about at the Lake House, uncaring of her plight.

Why did she feel such disappointment? Almost as if he'd betrayed her?

He owed her nothing. Had promised nothing.

Well, her petulant side, the side she usually kept subdued, complained, *if he hadn't insisted you stay at Perygrim Park, you wouldn't be in this awful situation.*

Not fair, her unbiased and logical side denied.

You could have asserted yourself. Refused to stay. You wanted to stay.

And there was the truth of it.

Eden had brought this catastrophe upon herself. She'd been weak. Had been beguiled by a pair of gray-green eyes and an unforgettable masculine face.

An unforgettable body too.

A flash of him standing in the moonlight, a glistening marble sculpture, plunged into her recriminations.

The miles passed quickly as she ruminated. She knew from the times she'd volunteered at the parish, handing out food and clothing to the poor, Vicar Wright rose early. Like she, he enjoyed gardening and usually spent an hour in his vegetable patch after breaking his fast. Four times he'd asked her to marry him since assuming the rectorship of St. Nicolas Priory two years ago. Every time she'd polity refused, and he'd given her a tender smile, vowing to persevere until she said yes.

Parking the dogcart before the church, she raised her eyes to the bell tower. This would be her life now. Not altogether unpleasant. Just not what she'd wanted.

In a few moments, Mrs. Bidwell, the parish's housekeeper, had shown Eden inside. Attired all in black with her hair pulled back into a severe, no nonsense knot, she marched along the dark corridor.

"Gracious, Miss Eden, you're out and about early today."

Too polite to ask directly, Mrs. Bidwell wore a mantle of curiosity as obvious as Vicar Wright's purple lent stole.

"Yes, I have errands to run and cannot be away from home too long. Mama's not well, so I left before she awoke."

Eden pulled her shawl firmer around her arms. The church was always cold inside. She supposed she'd get accustomed to that. She coughed into her handkerchief, fighting a wave of dizziness.

I cannot be sick.

"That cough sounds nasty, Miss Eden. You should be home in bed yourself." Mrs. Bidwell turned her gray-haired head, asking over her shoulder as she led the way to the small terrace at the rear of the rectory. "Is the Vicar expecting you?"

A bit of censure there. She knew he wasn't.

"No. I came about an urgent personal matter."

That sent the housekeeper's bristly eyebrows scurrying up her forehead. "Regarding your impending eviction, I presume?"

That halted Eden mid-step.

"I beg your pardon?"

"It's hardly a secret, dear. Everyone in Newbury knows."

No surprise really, but it still stung. Bitterly.

Either Simon or Lord Sterling had lost no time in spreading the news. If she had a crown to wager, she'd bet her brother had made certain her circumstances were made public. His lordship didn't seem the gossipy type.

What else had Simon blathered about?

Pray God not her foolhardy decision to spend the night at Perygrim.

Why, oh why, was I so rash?

Come to think of it, that might be why no one would consider her for a position. She'd ventured too close to the edge of ruin, and in the townspeople's view, she was a fallen woman.

Stupid. Stupid. Stupid Eden.

She'd destroyed everything on a feminine whim.

If only she'd never run into Lord Sterling.

"Vicar, Miss Eden is here to see you," Mrs. Bidwell announced at the terrace doorway.

Vicar Wright, a straw hat on his sandy brown hair, looked up from the row he'd been hoeing and gave a welcoming smile.

He really was an attractive man.

Even if he'd been as ugly as a hog, and as rotund and smelly as one as well, Eden would've accepted his offer.

"This is an unexpected surprise." He braced the

hoe against the vicarage. "Mrs. Bidwell, we'll take tea on the terrace here, please."

He indicated a quaint wrought iron table and chairs beneath an arbor covered with small white roses.

"If you've any of yesterday's delicious Bara Brith bread, I'm sure Miss Eden would enjoy a slice or two."

If her nervous stomach wasn't so wobbly, she might've. Bara Brith was a favorite indulgence, and only rarely did she have the opportunity to enjoy the treat.

A hint of disapproval tightening her mouth, Mrs. Bidwell nodded. "Of course, Vicar."

Eden commanded her nerves into submission and summoned a warm smile before coughing again.

"Pardon me."

After Mrs. Bidwell had disappeared inside, he waved Eden to one of the chairs, then collected his jacket and slipped it on.

"To what do I owe this pleasure?"

How did she approach something so delicate?

It would help if her stomach wasn't a gnarled lump and fever wasn't hindering her ability to parse her thoughts together.

Eden sank onto the chair and adjusted her shawl.

"I'm not quite sure where to begin."

"I've found the beginning is always the best place."

He gave her an encouraging smile, the corners of his dark brown eyes crinkling, revealing he smiled often.

Handsome and cheerful. She could do much worse.

"I'm sure you've heard about my . . . our change in circumstances."

He leaned back into his chair and nodded, a tinge of wariness settling over him. His expression and posture didn't change, but a guardedness she'd never seen before entered his eyes.

"Yes, a few parishioners have mentioned your difficulty."

Of course they had.

Felt it their Christian duty, no doubt, to apprise him of her reduced circumstances. Probably visited him *en masse* to make sure he knew every sordid detail, the judgmental chinwags. Nothing worse than a religious gossip. They never recognized their own sins for wont of pointing out others' iniquities.

She didn't even scold herself for her uncharitable thoughts.

It didn't help that for the first time Vicar Wright sat there regarding her in a manner that bordered on censure. She'd never known him to be anything but affable and considerate.

"I've been praying for you and your mother since I heard the news."

Well, that was something, but she needed much more from him.

"Thank you."

A silted silence descended upon them.

This was much harder than she'd anticipated. No sense beating around the bush.

Eden cleared her throat, both to dispel the nerves constricting it and to alleviate the soreness.

"I've carefully considered your offer and am pleased to say I accept."

Again, she forced her lips upward, husbanding a

semblance of happiness.

Eyes now hooded, he gazed blankly at her. Where he'd been relaxed and observant before, he now oozed strain.

"My offer?"

Good gracious, had he forgotten?

It had only been six weeks.

She swallowed against the soreness in her throat again and swept the area a quick glance. The last thing she needed was Mrs. Bidwell to overhear this awkwardness. As it was, the snoopy housekeeper was probably eavesdropping near the doorway.

Dread scraped along her spine. Eden clasped her hands until her fingers ached and quietly said, "Yes, your marriage proposal of a few weeks ago. If memory serves me correctly, it was the fourth."

She wasn't sure why she mentioned that tidbit. Maybe to reinforce the fact that he'd pursued her, not the reverse.

His countenance remained benign for a moment, then he turned his profile to her and sighed. He scratched his temple whilst looking at his robust garden.

"I regret I must retract my offer."

He'd heard.

"I see."

Could one perish from mortification?

He shook his head and finally met her eyes once more. His were full of compassion as well as accusation. "You see, I also learned you spent the night, unchaperoned, at Perygrim Park. After giving Lord Sterling a ride home. Also unchaperoned."

"What you say is true, but—" A fit of coughing interrupted her protest.

"I'm sure you can appreciate that a man in my position, a shepherd to his flock, cannot take to wife a woman of questionable repute. Therefore, I've no choice but to withdraw my former proposal."

Eden barely heard him. A fog descended over her mind, and she blinked several times to clear the haze floating before her.

So much for his declarations of love and adoration these past two years.

Withdraw my offer.

Her last option.

Except soiled dove or mistress.

A stunning young woman came around the corner of the rectory just then, holding each of his daughters' hands in hers. Wearing a smart pink and rose gown, the matching spencer edged in cobalt braid that just so happened to match the confection atop her perfectly coiffed golden curls, and her wide, pretty eyes, she gave him a winsome smile.

The immediate light flaring in his eyes told Eden all she needed to know.

He was not a man heartbroken. Not at all.

"Ah, you ladies haven't met yet." He stood and waved the three closer. "Miss Lucy Taylor, this is Miss Eglantina Haverden."

Had to use her given name, didn't he?

Couldn't even allow Eden a small degree of pride.

"Miss Eglantina, this is Lucy Taylor. Her father purchased the confectionary and mercantile last month, but she only arrived in town a fortnight ago."

"Don't forget the chocolate shop," Miss Taylor reminded him with another upward turn of her perfect mouth whilst blinking her ridiculously full lashes.

New to town and from a wealthy family. She'd replaced Eden in the vicar's attentions. Who'd choose a drooping dandelion when a lush rose was available for the plucking? He'd seized Eden's current bumblebroth to extract himself from his declaration.

Seven-year-old Emma bounced on her toes and grinned, revealing a missing front tooth. "Lucy is going to be our new Mama, Miss Eden."

Eden managed to find her way out of the church, coughing the whole while. Humiliation taunted her every step. Vicar Wright might've called her name. She couldn't be sure. It took every bit of her determination to remain upright and keep moving forward.

Crumpling into a defeated, sobbing mass was *not* an option.

Not in Newbury, leastways.

So great was her chagrin, she'd never be able to set foot in St. Nicolas Priory again.

Waves of burning heat then icy coldness engulfed her, over and over. She needed to get home. To lie down. To think of a solution.

There is no solution.

"Eden? Are you all right?"

Bloody perfect.

The cause of her downfall appeared before her, blurry and wavering. Right down to his immaculately polished Wellingtons.

"I cannot be seen with you, my lord. I'm disgraced as it is."

A fat tear seeped from the corner of her eye and trickled down her cheek.

He stepped nearer, and the smell that was him—masculine and intoxicating and dangerous for compromised spinsters—permeated the fog engulfing her.

"Eden, what has happened?"

"I beg you. Please go away."

She raised a shaky hand to her damp forehead. She was truly good and ill. And needed to sit at once.

Mouth pulled into a grim line, he shook his head. "I shan't—"

Everything went blissfully black.

9

Another three afternoons later, Chester stood outside Eden's bedchamber. Many were the times his feet—*mayhap his heart?*—had led him here since he'd brought her straight from Newbury. Most times, he'd summoned his waning diligence and discipline and walked on.

Other times, he couldn't resist seeing her.

More than once, he'd found her sleeping, convalescing from influenza, and he'd drawn up a chair and watched her slumber. Whether that made him a man well on his way to becoming utterly besotted or a lunatic, he couldn't say.

Was there much difference? Both had lost all

sense of reason.

At his insistence, Dr. Chamberlain visited each day, and he'd assured Chester she didn't ail from anything more dangerous than a severe case of ordinary grippe, made worse by her stressful circumstances, not enough to eat, and her unfortunate plunge into Black Beck.

Two uniformed maids hurried past, offering friendly smiles over the tall stacks of linens each carried.

Preparations for the house party were well underway. To Wynby's credit, he took to the task as if he'd organized many such gatherings. Additional staff had been hired, food and drink ordered, entertainment planned, and chambers that hadn't been used in years had received a thorough dusting and airing.

Chester rapped his knuckles once on the door.

"Come in."

Eden's lilting voice carried through the stout panel, sounding much more robust than she had yesterday when he'd checked on her.

He entered her chamber, mindful to keep the door

ajar to prevent further gossip.

Newbury had fairly crackled with conjecture and *on dit* his last visit. What was more, at least a dozen people had witnessed him carrying an insensate Eden to his coach.

Chester didn't even want to contemplate what the tattle-mongers were spreading about now.

Propped against pale pink sheets, a prim night robe buttoned to her chin and that mass of honey-toned hair flowing around her shoulders, Eden was speaking softly with her mother. Mr. Wiggles lay at the foot of her bed, and he gave Chester a single welcoming thud of his tail before shutting his eyes and resuming his slumber.

Today, he sported a purple ribbon about his scruffy neck.

Of Acorn there was no sign, but rustling in the adjoining sitting room suggested she was up to mischief of some sort. Luckily, on the day of the move from Briar Knoll, Chester had found her asleep in the sewing table. Several loops about the lid with a rope assured she'd remain in her nest until they reached

Perygrim. That was not to say Acorn went without creating a ruckus. Her outraged scolds and frantic clawing didn't cease until he released her in Eden's bedchamber.

Miss Haverden patted her daughter's hand and acknowledged Chester's entrance with a slight angling of her head. Her somber pecan brown eyes shimmered with gratitude.

"Your lordship, Eglantina's much improved. Thank you again for everything. You've been exceedingly kind, and we are grateful."

"You are most welcome."

His attention shifted back to Eden.

A touch more color brushed her gently sloping cheeks, and her eyes, now bright and focused, had lost the dull haze of fever. Indeed, she seemed far, far better than when she'd collapsed outside St. Nicolas Priory. He'd barely caught her in time to keep her from hitting her head upon the cobblestones.

"I hope you are improved as well, Miss Haverden."

"I am feeling immensely better, thanks to Dr.

Chamberlain's ministrations and treatment of my ill humors," Miss Haverden said whilst adjusting her shawl more securely around her frail shoulders. Life's difficulties had etched fine lines at the outer edges of her eyes and framed her mouth, but she was an attractive woman not even fifty years old yet.

According to Dr. Chamberlain, while Miss Haverden didn't boast a robust constitution, neither was she at death's door, as Chester had feared. She did possess delicate, easily frayed nerves, however.

Chester's disgust at learning Dr. Munson had cheated Eden and her mother had him struggling mightily with his ruthless inclinations. In addition to laudanum, the charlatan prescribed worthless nostrums and tonics and had the nerve to overcharge for what he'd termed *specialized* medicines, composed of ingredients that actually contributed to Miss Haverden's ill health.

Nonetheless, she'd rebounded remarkably in a short time, and a hint of healthy color now replaced her previous pallor. How much of that was due to the glass of sherry prescribed before bed each night, or the knowledge they were no longer indebted to Simon Andrews?

Or might her renewed vigor be due to his cantankerous father joining her in the solarium for tea these past two afternoons? Fully dressed to boot? Father preferred coffee, so his venture into socializing had a motive.

But what?

Chester had yet to determine what his sire was about, for he never did anything without purpose. On the other hand, to his relief, he and the duke had reached a truce of sorts. Much to his amazement—a tad of consternation too—Father hadn't objected to their unexpected guests either. Extraordinary considering his treatment of Eden the other night, and with the house party happening in mere days. Perhaps he'd taken seriously Chester's threat to leave and not return if he didn't make an effort to be more agreeable.

Yesterday, he'd moved back into his rooms at Perygrim. He couldn't very well leave the Haverdens to fumble about the place until Eden could be persuaded to become his secretary.

At least Dockery had taken his leave. Jervis too, the quisling. Not a doubt remained that the former bailiff had lined his and Dockery's pockets with Perygrim's profits during Father's decline in health.

Only the knowledge that Jervis and Dockery had families with young children prevented Chester from reporting them. Their children shouldn't have to suffer for their father's sins. The few pounds he offered in severance as well as a threat to notify the magistrate of their thievery encouraged them to leave peaceably.

"Mattie said you asked to see me?" He advanced farther into the room.

"Yes. I need to speak with you. Mama, I'd like a few minutes alone with his lordship, please."

"Of course, dear. I'm feeling a bit done in. I think I'll have a short lie down before dinner." She bent and kissed Eden's forehead and smoothed her hair. "I'm so glad you're feeling better. I was quite worried."

"I know, Mama. I truly am recovered."

Just a few days ago, their situations had been reversed, with Miss Haverden abed and Eden fussing over her. In both instances, their love for one another was obvious.

Something, perhaps sadness or regret, maybe even envy, tugged at his heartstrings. He didn't know how to overcome the frigid antagonism between the duke and him. Entrenched habits were not easily broken, especially when each was convinced the other was in the wrong.

Eden tugged the silk coverings higher on her lap as Chester approached the foot of the bed.

He'd have put her in the blue guest room.

The shades of cream, cobalt, and azure suited her color better than more vivid rose and plum hues of this chamber.

"I'll check in on you before I retire, darling," her mother said before sweeping from the room.

A full minute passed in silence after her departure, Eden staring into the corridor the whole while.

What troubled her?

With a deep breath, she directed her attention to him.

"Mama tells me you've moved the entire household to Perygrim, including our belongings, the chickens, bees, and Peony."

She sounded neither pleased nor angry.

Leaning a shoulder against the bedpost he nodded.

"I did. Even those special brocade or velvet or whatever they were rose bushes. It may have been presumptuous of me, but you were indisposed. Your mother as well as Mattie and Old Ronald were distraught when I called upon them to inform them you'd collapsed in the village."

In front of the church.

Why had she been there?

"You dug up the Blue Damask roses?"

When she looked at him like that, like he was her hero, her eyes soft and promising, he was hard put not to sweep her into his arms and profess his devotion.

"Indeed, I did." Because the confounded things were about to bloom, and he'd be buggered if he didn't do his part to make that legend of enemies becoming lovers a reality.

Specifically, this enemy.

"Old Ronald planted them in Mother's rose garden. He assures me they're thriving, and we can expect blossoms very soon."

"Thank you. That was very thoughtful." She seemed to collect herself, and her manner became more formal. "I'm sure you remember, tomorrow is the deadline for us to vacate Briar Knoll. There's something there I must retrieve."

"I would be happy to collect it for you."

He came 'round the side of the bed, then after a slight hesitation, sat by her hip. She'd lost weight. Not a lot, but enough to make her delicate features more pronounced.

"Honestly, I don't think you could find it."

"Very well, when you're fully recovered, we'll go together."

Her mouth twitched. "I'm well now, but Mama insisted I rest one more day. She's terrified of something happening to me."

He picked up one of her small hands. She didn't object but did slide a furtive peek toward the doorway. Cupping her hand, he brushed his thumb over the back.

"Unless I miss my mark, you were distressed when you came bolting out of the church the other day."

But why?

The question had simmered in the back of his mind for three days. If Pastor Perfect was Bible over bum in love with Eden, wouldn't he have called by now?

Her dainty fingers lying so comfortably in his palm went rigid, and she withdrew her hand.

"I hardly bolted, and as you know, I was ill. That's why you believed I was distraught."

"Why were you there?"

Preposterous to think this sickly feeling was jealousy.

Ridiculous he should dread her answer.

Ludicrous to deny he'd fallen in love with the vixen. That during the house party's ball, he yearned to announce that Eden was to become his wife before whisking her onto the ballroom floor for their first of many waltzes.

"That's none of your business, your lordship."

If she were a porcupine, she'd have shot him full of quills. "But since you're intent on prying, I sought his council on a position."

Chester would be bound the position she referred to was of a matrimonial nature and was no longer available.

"As it turned out, he wasn't able to help." Adept as she was at masking her feelings, her wounded eyes betrayed her.

Hmm. So, the Godly Gallant had fallen from grace.

"Do you want to know what I think, Eden, my sweet?"

"No. I do not."

Yes, distinct peevishness in her gimlet glance.

Leaning one elbow on his forearm, he rested his chin on his knuckles. "I think your chivalrous cleric threw you over. Vicar Valiant didn't possess the courage to stand up for the woman he proclaimed to love. I would, you know. The cost and stigma be damned."

"How very noble of you, considering you're the reason I'm disgraced." She sighed then and closed her eyes for a brief moment. "That was unfair, and you are right. He withdrew his offer. I cannot say I am surprised or that I blame him."

Chester wouldn't deny he was glad for it, though he ached for her humiliation.

"You would've married him even though you don't love him?"

She sank farther into the pillows, her expression defensive.

"Women have made greater sacrifices out of desperation."

Or love.

"Have you considered my offer to become my secretary?"

"I have, and I must decline. I appreciate your confidence in me, and that you are willing to cock a snook at decorum. But I confess, I am not so daring." There was that adorable wry smile. "I shall accept the housekeeper position if that is agreeable to you. Mattie says she'd rather remain Mama's companion. They've become fast friends. I realize I have no experience overseeing a household of this size, but I'm confident I can learn to do so. Toward that end, and because I'm burdening you with additional people and animals, I'll accept half wages."

To go from managing her own small home, the daughter of a man of means, to the role of a servant weighed heavily on her. He could see it in the merest downturn of her mouth and the fingers of her other hand clutching the coverlet.

Her pride wouldn't permit her to stay on as a guest either, though.

Even becoming Perygrim's housekeeper pushed the mark.

"All right. The position is yours. I'll inform my father. We can discuss wages later. Tomorrow, after we collect whatever it is you must have from Briar Knoll, I'll give you a tour of the house and we'll decide on appropriate compensation."

"I don't wish to overstep, but perhaps there are rooms we might use in the servant's quarters? Or . . ." She inhaled and ran the tip of her tongue along her bottom lip as if bolstering her courage. "Might Mama and Mattie live at the Lake Cottage? I would reside here, naturally. I don't wish to inconvenience his grace any more than we already have."

A nice way of saying she worried Father would bully her mother.

Such trust and faith shone in her eyes. Such cautious hope. He'd done nothing to earn it, but he'd cut off his own foot with embroidery scissors before betraying it.

He might've only known Eden Haverden for a few days, but his soul soared to think she'd be here, at Perygrim. Every day.

He'd see her every day.

Speak to her every day.

Giddiness bubbled behind his ribs.

Too soon to declare himself.

Did Eglantina Eden Haverden believe in love at first sight?

For he did now.

Chester released her hand as he contemplated her suggestion. He ran his fingers along his jaw. "I shall consider it. Why don't we see what happens for, shall we say, a fortnight?" He winked, and after a conspiratorial peek into the corridor, lowered his voice.

"Father's been taking tea with her."

Her mouth parted in astonishment, and she blinked at him, confused. "Together? And he hasn't been cross? She didn't say a word to me about it."

"I'm as astounded as you are, but I'd like to think it bodes well." Unable to resist a minute longer, he picked up one of her locks. It curled around his fingers, clinging to them like a vine taking possession of a wall or a tree.

"My lord . . ."

"Eden . . ."

He jerked his fingers away. "Pardon. Please continue."

She took another deep breath, an adorable blush pinkening her cheeks.

"I wasn't spying on you the other night at the lake."

"No? More's the pity. I quite hoped you were. I'd have been thoroughly compromised, and there's only one solution for that."

Too soon to broach that subject.

"Chester." She swatted his arm, eyeing him with

puckish regard. "Be serious. This is awkward enough. I want to apologize for intruding."

She'd used his given name. A chorus of hallelujahs hummed through his blood.

"No need for you to feel uncomfortable." He never wanted her to feel uneasy around him. He lifted a shoulder. "You couldn't have known I'd go for a swim. I'd just returned from London on a business matter with a bank I've invested in. There and back in two days, and I was desperate for a cool plunge."

"You were in London?"

Surprise, or maybe it was relief, skewed her winged brows together.

He nodded. "I was. I sent you a note."

Her silence and unwavering stare said what she did not.

Blister and blast it to Hades.

"You didn't receive it."

Not a question.

Docker and Jervis had already been dismissed. Which meant the footman he'd entrusted with the missive was too afraid of Father dismissing him to comply with Chester's request. Time to have a candid discussion with all the staff. Anyone who couldn't pledge loyalty to him would have to go. He'd not tolerate any more shenanigans.

He touched her cheek, grazing his fingers along the satiny skin, then cradled her jaw. She had such fine bones. Such a tempting mouth, which softened under his perusal.

With welcome?

"Did you think I'd reneged on my offer?"

She searched his eyes.

"Yes."

No excuses or accusation. Just the openness she'd always demonstrated with him.

"I'm sorry, sweet. Truly I am. I would've spared you the fretting. I'm not such a scapegrace that I'd give you false hope."

He leaned nearer, his entire focus trained on the delicate flare of her lips.

Her lashes fluttered closed.

A tender wisp of a touch at first.

Perfect and right and not enough.

She arched upward as he slid his hand behind her head, urging her closer.

Her lips parted at his gentle urging, and she released a ragged sigh.

Like a tippler desperate for his spirits, he eagerly tasted her honeyed mouth and explored the velvety softness.

Mr. Wiggles gave a worried whine, plummeting Chester back to earth.

Eden lifted an unsteady hand, and eyes wide and reproachful, touched her lips.

"My lord, I am your servant. Nothing else. If you ever kiss me again, I'll leave this house within the hour."

10

"What is so important that you have to set out yourself at eight o'clock in the morning?"

Lord Sterling's question stirred Eden from her reverie. She'd been reliving that delicious kiss of yesterday afternoon. Even now, she could feel his firm yet soft mouth on hers. She'd wanted more. Yearned to pull him down beside her and explore the contours of his face and well-muscled body.

More than carnal hunger swept her along on that river of desire. Chester had tunneled his way into her heart. Had captured it, good and well. That troubled her more than her wanton behavior.

Thank God Mr. Wiggles had interrupted.

Reality, cold and stark, had lanced her to the core, reviving a modicum of common sense.

She'd been on the verge of compromising herself with a man she scarcely knew.

Which made her wicked and fast.

Her behavior would shame Mama's. Dulcina had been unwilling, had been despoiled by Walter Andrews.

Eden, on the other hand, without so much as a finger lifted in resistance or a single objection, had melted into his arms, succumbing to the practiced rogue's skillful kisses. Worse, she well knew the consequences. Had she not lived three and twenty years, scorned and ridiculed because of her birth?

When had she become an utter nitwit?

Since meeting Manchester, Marquis of Sterling, future Duke of DeCourcy.

She flicked her fan open and waved it. The past two days had been unseasonably warm, which was why she wore a simple, short-sleeved morning gown, and her shawl lay unused on the seat beside her. But the rush of heat overwhelming her had nothing to do with the sun outside.

"Eden?"

"I really think you ought to address me more formally, since I am in your employ now."

She leaned against the carriage's plush burgundy squab and considered appropriate alternatives, all the while fluttering the fan. The conveyance fairly floated along compared to her dogcart. She'd better be careful, or she'd become accustomed to this luxury.

"What do you suggest?" he asked.

He didn't seem the least put off by her firm retort.

"Not Miss Haverden. That's how everyone knows Mama. Perhaps Mistress Eden or Mistress Haverden?"

"Mistress?" His voice went deep and velvety. Wholly mesmerizing. Wonderfully wicked. "An interesting notion."

The avid potency in his gaze—very much jungle green and slightly primeval as he lazily contemplated her—made her quiver to her toes.

A most stimulating and not at all objectionable quaking either.

Her gaze flew to his mouth, quirked into a

knowing smile. Then to his eyes, brimming with the thoughtful amusement she'd come to know.

Good God. He didn't think . . .?

He ought to be slapped for his impertinence.

She folded her arms across her chest, lest he see her unsolicited reaction.

Her mind and delicate sensibilities might object to his insinuation, but her young, healthy body most certainly did not.

As if he could read her tumbling thoughts, those probing eyes sank to her folded arms, and he chuckled whilst crossing his long legs.

"Eden, my sweet. All housekeepers are addressed as Missus. Even when they are unmarried. The staff will address you as Mrs. Haverden, as will Father. I promise to do so if anyone else is around."

"You will do so all the time, because you might be overheard. A man of your integrity would never risk bringing censure upon me by doing otherwise. That means no more calling me sweet and most assuredly no more kisses."

She had him there and couldn't contain the

jubilant twitch of her lips.

"*Hmm*, we shall see."

"I mean it, my lord. I must insist."

"Do you know your eyes turn almost indigo when you are peeved?"

"Nonsense." What rubbish.

"If you say so."

He glanced out the window and tensed. Alarm tightened his features. Grabbing the door, he leaned forward, swearing beneath his breath. He banged on the roof and shouted, "Simmons. To Briar Knoll. As fast as the team can go."

The carriage lurched forward, the powerful team of four racing over the track, and she nearly toppled from the seat.

"What's wrong?" Dread spinning her stomach, she scooted to the edge of the seat.

A dismayed cry ripped from her throat.

"No! No!"

Flames frolicked atop the cottage's peaked roof as Simon and what looked to be Dockery stood by. Tethered in the orchard, a pair of horses, heads raised and tails swishing nervously, shifted as they too watched the spreading fire.

Time crept along, each second stretching on and on before the carriage careened to a stop. Eden didn't wait for Chester to open the door or for the driver to lower the steps. She jumped to the ground, despair clogging her throat as she dashed to her brother.

She grabbed his arm, forcing him to face her.

"Simon. What have you done? We had a day left. Why would you do this?"

His glance held a modicum of pity. "You'd obviously vacated already. I told you'd I'd burn anything left."

"But I've been ill, and I didn't have a chance to make sure everything of importance was taken."

Her whole life, every memory, every celebration and milestone had occurred in the quaint cottage. He'd callously torched the only home she'd ever known. It was like losing a dear friend.

She stumbled forward a few steps, shaking her head. "Why burn the cottage? You could've let it to someone else."

Especially since she suspected he was short on funds

He cupped his nape. "I don't want the expense of repairing it, nor do I want to have to pay the taxes on the crumbling heap."

Or didn't want to risk she and Mama finding a means to return?

Lord Sterling came up beside her, and grasping her elbow, gently urged her away.

"There's naught we can do now, Eden. Come. Move away. It's not safe." The urgency in his gentle voice penetrated her shock, and as if drugged, she managed a slow nod.

"So, it's Eden now is it?" Simon's smirk implied all that he didn't say. "Dockery mentioned he'd seen you at Perygrim."

"Then he was trespassing, because I dismissed the cur for theft." Vehemence replaced the gentleness in Chester's voice.

Dockery quelled under the scorching glare Chester leveled him.

She gathered from his rapt regard, the churl

suddenly found the contorting shadows on the ground fascinating.

Chester whirled to the driver. "Go to Perygrim for help."

"Yes, sir." In a flash, Simmons vaulted into the driver's seat and set the team charging to the great house.

Not that it would do any good.

A tremulous child's whimper carried to her above the fire's roar.

"Auntie Egg?"

Premonition screeching a warning, she spun toward Prentice. Eyes huge and terror filled, he cowered by the empty chicken run.

"Prentice. What are you doing here?" Simon demanded from behind her. "I expressly forbade you to ever come here again."

"Prentice?" She ran to him.

Kneeling before her nephew, she gripped his small shoulders.

"Where's your brother? Tell me, Prentice. Where is Timothy?"

Lower lip trembling, he pointed to the cottage, the roof now completely engulfed in flames. "He went into the cottage. He said he wanted something to remember you by. Father said you were going away and we'd never, ever, *ever* see you again, Auntie Egg."

Oh no. Oh no!

Prentice collapsed against her, inconsolable.

Cradling his small, shuddering body fast against her, Eden on her knees, shifted to face Chester. Terror beat a brutal path from her heart to her lungs.

"Dear God. Timothy is inside the cottage."

"No. He cannot be." Simon stiffened and blanched.

The fire's unrelenting rage commanded her attention.

Timothy was in there.

"Oh God. He's inside that," she cried.

Simon whirled and seized Dockery by his collar, shaking him like a wild dog intent on breaking its prey's neck. "I told you to make sure no one was inside, you bloody imbecile. So help me, if anything happens to my heir, you'll regret ever approaching me for a position."

"I walked through all the rooms." Dockery yanked himself free, his lack of remorse stark and unforgiveable. "If the disobedient brat was hiding, it's no fault of mine."

With an infuriated growl, Simon planted him a facer.

Dockery folded to the ground in an unconscious heap.

Chester had already removed his jacket. He draped it over his head like a protective mantel.

Simon immediately did the same.

"I'll take the back entrance. You go in the front," Chester told Simon. "Stay as low as you can, and don't inhale the smoke. We've but minutes before the roof goes."

Eden closed her eyes as both men disappeared inside the inferno.

"God, please protect them. Let them find Timothy safe."

If she'd thought time inched by as they sprinted to the cottage, it now ceased to move at all. Every breath she took, every sob rattling Prentice's small body, every angry crackle and snap of the fire drew out endlessly.

Dockery roused and struggled to his feet. A vile sneer curled his lip as he brushed the back of his hand against his bloody nose.

Eden barely spared him a glance. She spoke into Prentice's hair. "Come on, Simon and Chester. Find Timothy. Hurry. You have to hurry."

Dockery mounted his horse, calling evilly as he galloped away, "I hope they all burn, the snobbish arses."

Minutes passed—Three? Five? More?

Bent over, wheezing and coughing, his hands clasping his chest, Simon staggered from the front entrance. He collapsed to his knees several feet away and covered his face with his hands.

"I couldn't find him." Rocking back and forth, he moaned, the sound so anguished and animalistic, Eden's flesh prickled. "I couldn't find my son. Oh God. What have I done?"

"Father?" Prentice whimpered. "Is my brother

going to die?"

He might already be dead.

Arms open wide, Simon silently beckoned his younger son.

Prentice ran to him and threw himself into his father's arms. They clung to each other, weeping.

Tears burned behind her lids as Eden tortured her lower lip, her hands pressed to her belly.

Where was Chester? He should have come out by now.

"Chester," she screamed, hugging herself. "Chester!"

She couldn't lose him too. Not when she'd admitted what he meant to her.

He couldn't remain inside much longer. The roof was going to cave in. No one could survive that.

Mind made up, she unfastened the frogs at her throat.

She had to try.

As she swung the cloak from her shoulders, Prentice cried out and pointed. "Look!"

She jerked her attention to the side of the cottage.

His face all grim angles and lines, Chester, holding Timothy, sprinted past where the rose bushes used to be. Timothy clung to him as he bolted away from the shuddering and groaning building.

"Timothy!" Simon scrambled to his feet, and as he lifted Prentice to his hip, ran to his son.

Chester lowered Timothy onto the grass.

The child lay back, coughing. Face crumpled and eyes squeezed shut, his small chest rose and fell rapidly as he strove to suck in fresh air.

Chester, too, lay sprawled on his back, one arm across his closed eyes. Smudges of soot covered his hands, and sparks had singed his shirt and trousers in several places.

His dear face too.

Eyes overflowing, Eden dropped to her knees beside them. She pressed a kiss to Timothy's reddened cheek.

"My darling, I'm so very, very glad you are safe."

Simon squatted next to his son and touched his cheek just below a penny-sized burn.

"I'm sorry I disobeyed you, Father." Lower lip

quivering, Timothy did his utmost to be a stoic little fellow. "I know I deserve to be punished."

"I'm the one who's sorry, son. I've been such a bitter fool, and I almost lost you."

Simon swiped at the wetness on his face as he gathered his son into his arms.

"We'd best move farther away." Chester labored to stand, and Simon offered him his hand.

After the merest hesitation, Chester accepted his assistance.

Eden picked Prentice up, and Simon gathered Timothy in his arms. They hustled across the lane to the orchard beside Simon's nervous mount. They'd no sooner turned to look at the fully engulfed cottage than the roof gave way, shooting sparks and flames skyward ten feet or more

"I owe you a debt of gratitude, Sterling."

So formal and stiff. Simon didn't look at Chester.

Even now, when his son had almost died because of his petulance, was his pride preventing him showing genuine appreciation? Would he have done the same for Chester if their positions had been reversed?

Eden would've liked to think Simon would, but frankly, she doubted it.

Chester had risked his life for the son of the cur who had killed his brother. No question who the better man was. A scrumptious warmth spread from her heart outward. Had their circumstances been different, Chester was a man she could've loved.

Did love, though he'd never know it.

How different Simon and Chester were. Though both had similar backgrounds and education, Chester had chosen the nobler path whilst Simon stuck to his rigid protocols.

"I'm relieved he's all right. Nonetheless, I'd have a physician examine him, Andrews. He has a few burns, and he inhaled smoke."

Chester untied his neckcloth. He wiped his face, wincing when he encountered the raw places.

At last Simon dragged his attention from the burning cottage. He looked between Eden and Chester, a tinge of his former haughtiness appearing.

"If the offer to join the house party is open, I will inform my wife we are to attend."

His enthusiasm matched that of a person about to have their coffin nailed shut. Nevertheless, he'd made an effort. That was something.

Chester inclined his head. "I'll have an invitation delivered tomorrow."

How would the Duke of DeCourcy take the news? His nemesis within Perygrim's walls?

Perhaps Wynby ought to remove anything that could be used as a weapon including hairpins and toothpicks. Pickle forks too?

"I'd better see my sons home." Simon lowered Prentice to the ground before untying his horse.

"Dr. Chamberlain is supposed to call at Perygrim at one o'clock. I can have him stop at Gablecrest when he is done," Eden said as she pulled her nephews into her arms.

"I would appreciate it." Simon nodded as he mounted. "Sterling, I can hold Prentice before me, if you can lift Timothy behind me."

In a trice, the three sat atop the patient roan.

Prentice grinned, bending to peek at his brother.

"We've never ridden with Father before, have we

Timothy?"

There were a great many things the boys had never done with their father.

For an instant, Simon appeared flummoxed. He looked over his shoulder at Timothy, then at Prentice's upturned face.

"Is that something you would enjoy?"

"Yes, Father." The boys nodded eagerly.

If Simon finally started being a loving father to his sons, then Briar Knoll burning to the ground was worth it.

"Walk on, Reuben." He clicked his tongue and gave a final nod while the boys waved farewell.

Eden watched them until they were out of sight. Reluctantly, she focused on the fire once more. The cottage was so old and shabby, the fire was quickly reducing it to rubble.

"Are you all right?" Chester laid a broad hand on her shoulder.

"I should be asking you that."

"I'm fine. Just a few small burns. This though . . ." His gaze swept the blazing building. "You must be devastated."

A distraught, strangled laugh echoed amongst the trees, and it shocked her to realize it was she who was cackling like a madwoman.

"The agreement between my mother and Walter Andrews was wrapped in an oil cloth and hidden atop one of the rafters."

"That's what you came for?"

Chester slung his cravat over his shoulder before draping an arm across hers and drawing her into the protective crook of his chest, smelling of sweat and fire.

"It was."

Two nights ago, she'd awoken in the early morning hours, a long-forgotten memory jarring her awake. Now she'd never know the truth of it.

He kissed her crown, his warm breath in her hair, comforting. "Is it really such a loss, since you've already decided on a new course?"

Something odd in the timbre of his voice gave her pause, and she angled her head to better examine his face. Did he worry she'd changed her mind about becoming Perygrim's housekeeper? For certain, the position wasn't her first choice, but when a person was reduced to nothing, they couldn't be particular.

At least now she knew everyone would be fed and have a warm place to sleep.

If his grace became difficult, she'd have to reexamine the situation.

"I'm not sure, honestly. It's been eight years since I briefly scanned the document. Most of the language was meaningless legal mumbo jumbo. But one clause in particular confused me. I can't be sure, of course, but I believe it inferred that if ever Mama and I were put from Briar Knoll, a sum was to be settled upon us."

Chester made a rough sound in his throat.

"Did your brother know of the clause?"

"I don't know that either. I do know he, or someone he hired, ransacked the cottage more than once while we were attending church services before Mama became too ill. Nothing was ever stolen, but I always wondered if he was after the agreement. If only there was another copy."

She shrugged and nestled a tiny bit closer. Why

couldn't she be brave enough to wrap her arms around his waist?

What happened to no more kisses?

He was her employer.

He couldn't be anything more.

"It matters naught now," she said. "If it had been true, I'd still have had to hire a solicitor. I could offer him part of the settlement in payment, I suppose. I always wanted to accompany Mama to Bath so she could take the waters. It's been her lifelong dream to live near the ocean."

It hadn't escaped her either that while Simon had said he'd attend the duke's house party, his newfound agreeableness didn't extend to Eden or her mother. There'd been no offer of help, no inquiry as to what their plans were.

The rejection wasn't new, yet it stung.

Chester turned her so that she was fully within his soothing embrace: chest-to-chest and thigh-to-thigh.

She could stand like this for hours.

He tightened his arms about her. "It's impossible. I shan't let you go."

"I beg your pardon?" She angled away to look up at him.

He was silent for a long moment, then sighed. "You committed to becoming Perygrim's housekeeper, and we're having a house party soon. Are you going to break your word now?"

Was he serious?

For a foolish instant she'd thought he'd meant something more . . . romantic.

Her childhood home was engulfed in flames.

Her nephew had nearly died, and he was disgruntled because he believed she wanted to leave?

He didn't even know if she'd be a capable housekeeper. She didn't know if she would either. Which frightened her, because that was truly her last respectable resort.

She firmed her mouth. "My lord—"

"Chester," he corrected, entwining a hand in her hair while something as hot and potent as the fire behind her flared in his gaze.

Oh no, you don't. I'm not falling for that again. I may have lost my heart, but my virtue is intact.

Summoning her most professional mien, she refused to allow him to see how he affected her. "I'm grateful for the position, but even you must realize it's not my first choice."

"What would be your first choice, Eden?" His gaze deepened, holding her reluctant attention. "If you could have your heart's desire, have any wish granted, what would it be?"

He kissed her nose, the act so tender and endearing, tears threatened.

Why did it have to be this man who penetrated her heart? Who was able to make her feel all the things she couldn't for Vicar Wright? A man far beyond her reach?

"I know what mine is," he murmured.

He kept wrapping her hair around his hand, drawing her face closer and closer to his until only a couple of inches separated their mouths.

And of course, though she ordered her gaze to stay locked with his, the dratted, traitorous thing dipped to his sculpted lips. Lips she craved to taste again.

This was dangerous, sharing innermost secrets. A

ridiculous game of fancies and dreams. It spoke of an intimacy forbidden to her.

He was the next Duke of DeCourcy.

She was his bastard housekeeper.

It didn't take a scholar to decipher the obvious.

"I'll go first," he said, tracing a finger from her ear, along her jaw, and to her chin, which he gently tipped upward. "My greatest wish is that *you* have *your* greatest wish."

Could he have said anything more unselfish? More moving? More perfect?

Another layer of self-protection crumbled.

She opened her mouth to respond but no words came forth.

What could she say?

That her greatest wish was to be with him? Forever?

Then his mouth was on hers again, and she forgot her vows to remain aloof and impervious to him. Forgot she was beneath his touch and that she could never hope for more.

Whether it was the scare he'd had earlier, or that

he'd lost hold of the rigid restraint keeping his passion in check, she couldn't say. He was like a man long starved, holding her face in both hands, raining kisses over her eyes and cheeks and mouth.

He released her face and gripped her bottom with one hand, lifting her into the rigid hardness pressing into her belly, and at the same time cupped her head, angling it so he had access to her neck and chest. The low bodice of her simple gown gave him access to much more.

His lips met hers again, and such a rush of sensation ambushed her, her knees came unhinged. She opened her mouth to his ravenous onslaught, finding an answering hunger billowing through her.

"Eden, say you'll be mine," he whispered against her cheek. "I know you want me as much as I want you."

That cooled her rampant ardor.

She must make him understand; she would never be any man's plaything.

Never.

"My lord, aren't you forgetting about Miss Bickford? Your soon-to-be betrothed?"

11

Another fortnight passed as Eden quickly learned her duties as Perygrim's housekeeper. She'd expected resentment and resistance from the other staff but found them to be cooperative and helpful.

How much had Chester to do with that?

All the staff had been present when she'd been introduced, and he'd made it clear that anyone unwilling to be one hundred percent loyal to him would be dismissed.

He'd assured her acceptance despite his annoyance with her.

Reminding him of the heiress he was expected to wed as Briar Knolls's walls crumbled had served its purpose. She'd been rewarded for her cleverness when his eyes flashed in exasperation, but he'd released her without another word. Or kiss.

And yet, she couldn't get his softly murmured words out of her mind.

My greatest wish is that you have your greatest wish.

Neither could she ignore the flicker of delight recalling them caused.

The chatelaine clinking against her hip and the rustle of her prim dark blue gown were accompanied by the *click-click* of Mr. Wiggle's paws as he followed her on her daily rounds. She wore one of five new garments that had arrived yesterday. They'd been accompanied by stockings, shoes, and undergarments.

How Chester had managed to have them made so swiftly, she didn't inquire, but she had asked how he'd acquired her measurements.

He'd given her a sheepish grin and confessed to taking her ivory and jonquil frock to use as a pattern.

The gown might be a servant's simple trappings, but the material and expert sewing spoke to its quality.

Silly as it might be, the plain gown boosted her confidence a smidgeon. She'd not needed to fear the duke's guests would find fault with her appearance.

The visitors would begin arriving the middle of next week, including Miss Bickford. Chester continued to vow he had no interest in wedding his father's choice as the next duchess.

Perusing her to-do list, she risked a small frown.

His grace insisted the gathering was an intimate party—a mere forty of the most prominent members of the *haut ton*.

She'd commit some gaffe, she had no doubt.

She swept into the library, checklist in hand. A package had arrived yesterday, which included, amongst other things, the latest novels popular amongst the upper Ten Thousand. Lifting one volume, she chuckled and pulled a face.

"*Frankenstein*. I should think I'd have nightmares upon reading it."

"You aren't the only one."

Chester—*no, he's Lord Sterling*—lounged against the library entrance. He waggled his eyebrows at her, and giving her one of his rakish smiles, sent a kaleidoscope of butterflies flitting about her insides.

"I must say, you're the most fetching housekeeper I've ever laid eyes upon."

The largeness of his presence made the grand paneled room seem much smaller.

She arched a brow and firmly ignored the winged creatures cavorting in her middle.

Respectable housekeepers should not indulge in naughty fantasies about their employers.

"Did you need something, my lord?"

"Chester," he whispered sotto voce with a naughty wink. He lifted a shoulder. "I needed to see you. You've been avoiding me. I've missed your smiles."

His hooded eyes suggested he'd missed more.

She had been dodging him. For both their sakes.

Any more of his devastating kisses, and she'd be undone for certain.

This morning, she'd ducked behind the draperies in the study.

Yesterday, she'd sequestered herself in a linen closet, and the day before, she dove behind the settee in the drawing room. That had proved rather awkward when she clambered up to find Wynby gaping at her. She'd claimed to be inspecting the undersurface of the settee for rips.

He'd drolly commended her diligence.

Nevertheless, she encountered Chester a dozen or more times a day. She swore he lay in wait for her, and she'd taken to peeking around corners before entering rooms.

He also seemed set on courting her.

There'd been a rose upon her pillow two afternoons—not the Blue Damask, but a lovely coral, and a yellow with ruby edges. Chocolates twice too. She'd found notes tucked in her apron pocket and beneath her pillow. There'd also been a book of poetry with several pages marked.

All love sonnets.

Who would've thought the formidable Marquis of Sterling was such a romantic?

Several times he'd sought her out on some trivial matter. He'd touch her elbow, the small of her back, tuck a wisp of hair over her shoulder, and each time, her awareness of him grew as a virile man who very much wanted her.

He was slowly, oh, so expertly, drawing her into his web.

She'd be a liar if she denied it thrilled as much as frightened.

Tamping down her happiness at seeing him, she ran her forefinger down the list. "I haven't time to chat. I've an awful lot to accomplish before your guests arrive."

"As I told you days ago," he said, straightening to his full height, "they, including Miss Bickford, are Father's guests. Not mine. I'm simply humoring an elderly man's wishes."

A flush swept her, and she made a pretense of arranging the novels on a low, marble-topped rosewood table so the guests wouldn't have to search for them. Chester had finally convinced her he truly had no intention of honoring his father's request to wed Miss Bickford. It oughtn't make her happy, but it did—absurdly so—nonetheless.

Poor Miss Bickford. She was in for a tremendous

disappointment if she'd set her cap for Chester.

So was the duke, and that worried Eden more than a little.

While his grace was polite, not cordial by any means, but not the hostile man she'd first met, she'd caught him watching her, a steely, calculating glint in his eye. He continued to take tea with Mama every day, and Eden feared Dulcina had formed an attachment to the duke.

"My lord, might I speak candidly?"

He stopped fiddling with the ivory elephant he'd been holding and, after placing it back on the side table, advanced toward her. "Always. What is it?"

"I fear my mother may be developing a *tendre* for his grace. I think it would be best if she and Mattie moved to The Lake House before it goes any further."

Should she stack the books upright or lay them side-by-side?

He cocked his head, a slight frown veeing his brows.

"You don't think your mother deserves to care for someone?"

"That's not what I mean at all. She's a disgraced governess, and he's a duke." She glanced at her lengthy to-do list. How was she to ever get all that done by Friday? Should she assure the bedchambers were all readied or ask Old Ronald about when to best cut the flowers for the myriad of vases she wanted filled with bouquets? "But nothing can come of it. Their stations are too distant."

He scratched his ear, giving her a boyish grin.

"I don't know. Father's mellowed dramatically since Miss Haverden's arrival. In truth, I haven't ever seen him as amiable. I'll admit I'm glad for it and the effort he seems to be making. Dr. Chamberlain says the company has done his health good. Would you deprive your mother and my father the enjoyment?" He rested a hip on the edge of a writing desk. "Why don't we wait and see how things play out?"

She sighed and looked to the ornate ceiling and husbanded her patience.

Why was he being so obtuse?

"Naturally, I want them to be happy." *Was such a thing even possible for the duke?* "But I cannot bear to see my mother hurt anymore. How could his grace possibly return her regard? You know as well as I that peers only trifle with those beneath their station."

"Is that what you think of me too? That I'd play with your affections then toss you aside like an old, worn shoe?" His stern regard held her captive.

How dare he get his bristles up?

"Sir, *I* am living, breathing proof of that very thing."

How had this turned into an argument between them?

Because passion bubbled beneath the surface, and if it couldn't be appeased one way, it would be another.

He towered over her now. Not threateningly, but powerful and commanding, and not easily dismissed.

"No, you are not. Your mother didn't have any affection for Andrews. It's not the same at all. When two people care for each other, love each other above all else, station does not matter."

"What do you know about it? You who've never had to ignore barbed comments and sly looks? Never had to pretend indifference while simmering with embarrassment." She flung her hair behind her. "Never had to wonder where your next meal would come from?" She slammed the last book down then lowered her voice, fearful someone would overhear their argument. "Are you saying none of your elite acquaintances have taken advantage of their lofty positions to have their way with a servant or other woman who caught their roving eye?"

"I cannot deny that, nor can I tell you what's going on inside my Father's head. But I vow I am not like them, and I take exception to you lumping me in with the likes of those cretins. I have fought seven duels for that very reason. Duels against those who are deemed my social equals, because they abused their position and ruined an innocent without remorse. Those are the keys, Eden. Deliberate intent and lack of remorse."

He plowed his long fingers through his thick hair and paced to the window seat. His shoulders rose and fell in his agitation. He sliced her a hard glance over his broad shoulder.

"And you, Eglantina Eden Haverden, are as much a snob as they are if you restrict love and affection to those in the same social class. I'd have thought better of you. Love can happen at any time, between anyone, and it's a gift to be treasured."

He looked at her with such disappointment, chagrin beset her. Shaking his auburn head, he spun on his heel and stalked to the library door.

"By the by, Father insists you wear your hair up when *our* guests are here."

Stinging sarcasm that.

"He won't budge on the matter, though I tried to dissuade him."

Eden remained rooted to the floor. The order to tie her hair up hadn't rattled her. She'd expected it sooner, truth to tell.

Chester's confession about the duels had dissolved her irritation.

He'd risked his life several times for a woman's reputation?

She'd misjudged him.

She swallowed and blinked back tears before

collecting her list and examining the blurry entries.

What to do next?

Oh, yes. Chef wanted a word about dainties and cakes to serve during teas.

"Mrs. Haverden?"

His grace rolled his invalid chair into the library.

How could she not have heard his approach?

A certain marquis's striking features floated to mind as she bobbed a curtsy.

She may have been a trifle distracted.

"Your Grace."

Where was Neville?

As if reading her mind, the duke said, "I sent Neville to the kitchen for my coffee. Did you know he's the father of eight?"

"No, I was not aware." She folded her list and, after tucking it into her apron pocket, offered a polite smile. Since her arrival, his grace's health seemed more robust as well. Mayhap Chester was right. "May I be of help?"

Is that what she was supposed to say?

"I wanted a private word with you. I heard you

arguing with my son."

Eavesdropping, was he? How much had he heard?

She firmly disregarded the heat sweeping over her cheeks.

"That won't do, you know. I expect the lower orders to know their place. Any further breaches and you will be dismissed at once."

His smile held no warmth as he flicked his cold gaze over her, lingering for a moment on her unbound hair.

This was the true Duke of DeCourcy. The blackguard was play-acting with Mama, she'd vow. To what purpose?

"I understand. It won't happen again, Your Grace."

Eden clasped her hands behind her back. She'd not give the spiteful curmudgeon the pleasure of seeing her undone.

Fingers steepled, he nodded.

"Good. Good. Oh, and if you've any imprudent designs on my son, you'd best rid yourself of those foolish notions. I only permitted him to hire you so he'd move back into the big house. I have a duchess selected for him. He *will* marry Miss Bickford."

Eden lifted her chin in proud defiance. "I'm sure his lordship knows his own mind."

"Stupid, stupid green girl. What he wants is of no importance. It's what I want that counts. I am the duke, not he." He jabbed his thumb at his chest. "Manchester will propose, or my guests will be dismayed to find valuables have gone missing. I have loyal servants in this household."

Like Neville? Father of eight? Who couldn't afford to be jobless?

"As there's never been any prior incidences of thievery at Perygrim, who else will the magistrate suspect but the newest members of the household?" he asked, with unnerving calm. "Naturally, the stolen goods will be discovered in your and your mother's possession."

The oatmeal Eden had eaten at half past six this morning threatened to reappear.

"You would not dare."

Yes, the duke would.

He practically exuded glee. He'd orchestrated everything. Expertly played everyone like ivory pieces on a chess-board.

"Manchester would never let you and your mother go to prison. He's too bloody noble." He curled his lips in disgust. "He loves you too much, the damned sentimental fool. Just like his mawkish mother."

He loves me?

Oh, if only it were true.

"What makes you think I won't tell his lordship about your scheme?"

"I've already planted jewels and other trinkets. Even now, I have someone prepared to *find* them. I have only to say the word." He drummed his bony fingers on the chair arms. "Why, think of it. You could be sitting in a cold, dark, rat-infested cell within hours."

Eden hugged her shoulders.

The duke was an evil fiend. No matter what she did, someone she loved was going to suffer.

Her breath stalled in her lungs as the truth hit her.

Chester was right.

It didn't matter who you were. How long you'd known someone. What station they were. Love was oblivious to all of those things.

How could she choose between him and Mama?

Mama *would* die in prison.

"You either watch the man you love wed another woman or send your mother to prison for life. With her frail health, she'll be gone within weeks. You, however, are made of sterner stuff. You'll last years and years, I'll be bound."

His cruel cackle ended on a harsh cough.

Jaw clenched, she glared at him.

"Of course, once Manchester proposes to Miss Bickford, I'll want you gone. I'll even give you a thousand pounds to take your mother, servants, and that ratty dog and disappear. Forever."

12

Chester stalked down the corridor, Wynby and Neville marching behind him. He held a purple velvet bag, jingling with jewels and small pieces of silver Neville was to have hidden in Eden and Miss Haverden's chambers.

He'd gone to Wynby instead.

Father had gone too far, conspiring to incriminate Eden and her mother. By God, Chester would find out why.

He loosened the bag's tie, then lifted a handful of the gems.

Mother's.

A sapphire and diamond ring glittered atop the

pile, the square cut gem nearly the same unusual pale blue as Eden's eyes.

A smile teasing the corners of his mouth, he pocketed the ring before returning the other jewels to the pouch.

At the foot of the stairs, he lifted his hand.

"I'll continue to the library alone. I cannot express my gratitude to either of you. Your loyalty is commendable, and rest assured, Neville, you will always have a position in this house. You'll find my temperament much more moderate than my sire's."

"Thank you, sir." Tangible relief relaxed Neville's plain features. He'd risked much betraying the duke.

"Go below stairs, and keep the other staff there as well," Chester said, balancing the bag on his palm. "I'll summon you when I need you."

The servants exchanged a knowing look as they continued down the corridor.

Once Chester had wrangled his ire under control, he proceeded to the library, treading on silent feet. He'd truly wanted to attempt a reconciliation with the duke, but this latest stunt revealed the futility of any such effort.

"I shall not accept a pence from you, sir. And if you think your offer of money will keep me silent while you manipulate your son, you've made a strategic miscalculation. Not only will my mother and I leave this house at once, I believe Lord Sterling will thwart any attempt you make to frame us for theft."

"Indeed, I certainly shall."

Chester entered the library.

As he closed the door, a guilty flush tinged his sire's cheeks. Chester crossed to the duke and dropped the bag into his lap, relishing his flabbergasted expression.

"Why is it I'm not surprised you'd stoop to such depths, Father? What I don't know is why you want to frame Eden?"

"Because he wants to force you to marry Miss Bickford." Eden's contempt was palpable as she clasped her hands.

Chester rubbed his nose when what he wanted to do was sweep her into his arms and march out the door, through the foyer, and straight to the stables, where they'd bundle into a coach and make straight for Gretna Green.

"I fail to see what one has to do with the other." He touched the hard-little lump in his pocket instead.

Soon.

"Stop being obtuse, Manchester," the duke snapped. He scowled at the bag. "I knew you'd never allow the chit or her mother to go to prison. I was simply insuring you'd propose. I want to see my grandson before I die. I'm not a well man."

"You're also not dying as you led me to believe, are you, Father?" Chester had learned that tidbit his first day home. "In fact, Dr. Chamberlain says you don't need that invalid chair at all, and liberally applied rice powder can be credited for your sickly pallor."

That rendered the duke blessedly mute.

"Please excuse me, I need to pack."

Eden squared her shoulders and lifted her chin with a duchess's aplomb. She was as angry as he'd ever seen her.

"Can I impose upon you to wait a few moments

more?" Chester smiled at the haphazardly arranged books. Decorating was not Eden's forte. "I have something to say you should hear."

She scrunched her nose in that adorable way she had when puzzled, then after searching his face in the assessing manner he'd become accustomed to, gave a short nod.

"All right."

He cupped an elbow in his palm and rested his chin on his other fist.

"If I understand correctly, Father, if I concede to your wishes and propose, you'll settle one thousand pounds on Eden?"

A tiny flicker of shrewdness entered his father's eyes. He glanced between Eden and Chester several times.

"That's correct."

"Rather a stingy offer, I think." Chester cocked his head as he brushed a bit of lint from the jewelry bag off his lapel. "Make it five thousand pounds, and include a house at the seashore, and I'll agree."

Eden's stifled gasp nearly ripped his heart from

his chest.

She averted her face, but not before he saw the shocked tears pooling in her periwinkle gaze. "Don't be—"

"I agree. I agree. A house and five thousand. But she goes today." Father pointed a spindly finger at Eden. "I can't risk you changing your mind. We'll have to manage the house party with the extra help. Perygrim's been without a housekeeper this long and we've got on well enough. Viscountess Bickford has already agreed to act as hostess in any event."

I'll bet she has.

"I'll have your word on that, Father. Swear to it. And that you'll never harass Eden or her mother again. And that includes any sort of threat or blackmail."

His father might be a good many ignoble things, but his word was his oath. Chester had never known him to break it.

"I swear on Byron's grave."

Triumph glittered in Father's eyes and curved his mouth. He all but licked his lips in jubilation.

"If you think your heroics are necessary, my lord,

they are not. Do not sacrifice yourself for me." Eyes shooting sparks of accusation, Eden pivoted toward the doorway. Head high, spine stiff, she unpinned the chatelaine. "I told your father and I'll tell you. I will not accept a cent. I cannot be bribed."

With that, she dropped the chatelaine on a table. She flung her glorious hair over her shoulder as she swept to the door.

Chester rushed after her, blocking her way. He caught her hand. "You misunderstand, sweet."

"I don't think I do." She tried to shake him off. "Please release me."

"In a moment." He leaned nearer as he drew the ring from his pocket. "I want to ask you something first."

He slipped the ring on her finger.

Confusion combined with hope blossomed across her features.

"Chester?"

"What's going on?" His father tried to turn his chair but a wheel had become stuck on the rug. Instead, he craned his neck. "Let the gel go. Good riddance, I say. I've had enough of Andrew's spawn in my house."

"On the contrary, Father. I'm doing as you bid. I'm proposing. Oh, and I believe I forgot to mention, Simon Andrews will be attending the house party. I, on the other hand, will not."

"The devil you say?"

Father collapsed back into his chair, staring at Chester as if seeing him for the first time.

Clasping Eden's hands, Chester dropped to one knee.

"Eglantina Eden Aster Haverden, the moment you plowed into me at the Fox and Falcon, I knew you were something special. And with each passing day, each hour, every minute, I've become more besotted, more entranced, and more convinced that I want to spend the rest of my life with you. I adore you. Will you marry me?"

"What?" Father's strangled objections sounded like something between a rooster crowing and a sheep's bleating. He pushed to his feet. "No. No. I forbid such a misalliance. You must propose to Miss

Bickford."

Brow quirked, Chester glanced behind him.

"I never mentioned a woman's name. I only agreed to propose. And I've done so, as you've witnessed. I shall hold you to your oath." He spared the duke no quarter. "You are done manipulating me and others. Any children I father will be with this precious woman, if she'll have me."

Chester returned his attention to Eden, regarding him with such tenderness, moisture stung his eyes.

"Come with me." He grabbed her hand and led her through adjoining doors, then into the rose gardens.

Amid the backdrop of blooming roses, he gathered her into his arms and pressed a kiss to her welcoming mouth. "Say you'll marry me, Eden. I do love you. More than I even knew I could love anyone. I've waited a lifetime for you."

"Are you positive, Chester?" She hugged his waist, her head resting against his chest. "Even knowing who I am? Even knowing your father is set against it?"

He tipped her chin up. "My mother was a wise

woman. She said if I were ever lucky enough to find a woman I loved more than life itself to toss everything else aside to be with her. So, yes, Eden. I am absolutely sure."

Her gaze strayed to the doors they'd just exited. "I cannot live here."

"Neither can I. We'll go to the seashore. There's a ducal estate near Brighton." He kissed her nose. "Yes, you can have your chickens and bees and Peony. As bitter as my father is now, I pray when the grandchildren begin arriving—and I hope we have a passel—he'll come around."

Eden stood on her toes and wrapped her arms around his neck, pulling his head down until their lips met. She kissed him, and as her soft mouth moved beneath his, Chester's heart burgeoned with joy.

He had his answer.

Breathless, her eyes glowing, she touched his face.

"Yes, Chester. I'll marry you."

"Eden? Look." He rotated her until she saw what he'd spied. Almost reverently, he snapped the blossom from the bush and presented it to her. "It's an omen.

I'm sure of it."

She smiled into his eyes. "The first Blue Damask rose to bloom in decades. It's as if some force knew we were meant to be together."

"Indeed, my love. And who am I to argue with a legend?"

Epilogue

Brighton, England
August 1823

Eden leaned back into Chester's embrace as they observed the future Duke of DeCourcy and his grandmama playing in the gardens. Behind them, Old Ronald tended the flowerbed dedicated to the Blue Damask roses.

"Byron darling, come away from the fountain," Mama said as Mr. Wiggles tried to herd the determined auburn haired, blue-eyed baby toward his Grandmama.

Mattie laughed and picked up the sailor cap Byron had lost whilst running from them.

"Goggy," Byron giggled, digging his pudgy fingers into Mr. Wiggle's fur.

Mr. Wiggles promptly flopped onto his back, all four feet in the air, and proceeded to wiggle in the manicured grass, which sent Byron into another round of hysterical giggles.

"Can you believe he's almost two years old already?"

Eden tilted her head to meet Chester's eyes.

"No, I cannot. A note arrived from Father this morning saying he'd be here by week's end for the celebration. I think naming our son after Byron finally bridged the chasm, and he was able to let go of the past."

"That and forbidding him to see our son until he'd apologized for his awful conduct and showed he was truly repentant." To the duke's credit, his behavior had markedly improved.

Chester patted her tummy and nuzzled her nape.

Her birthmark no longer embarrassed her—how could it when Chester loved to kiss her there? She'd taken to wearing her hair up, especially when Byron thought it funny to grab fistfuls if she left it down.

"And soon, there will be another cherub for his grandparents to dote over." Chester kissed her neck again.

"Oh, this baby's a girl. I can tell." Eden framed the small mound with her hands. "Simon, Candace, and the boys are coming too, by the way. It was truly generous of you to advance him the monies to invest in sheep ranching. Candace says the woolen mill is doing well too. I can rest easier now knowing their financial reverses are on the mend."

"Only because I control everything he does at this juncture. I'm confident in time, he'll be able to stand on his own two feet once more." Chester nipped her ear, sending another delicious spark to those places he was so accomplished at exploring.

"Come with me." She seized his hand, and with a quick glance to make sure Mama had Byron well in hand, pulled her husband into the house.

"What are you about, sweet?

He knew full well.

She laughed at the wicked grin he gave her.

In a trice, they'd reached their chamber, and without preamble stripped away their clothing. The cool air was most welcome.

Chester lifted her, and as he carried her to the bed, nibbled her neck, his tongue flicking out and touching that sensitive spot that turned her brain to mush.

"Hurry, Chester."

"Eager are you, sweet?"

He grazed a kiss across her breast as he hooked her knee over his hip and slid home. "Better, love?"

Eden groaned as she moved against him, "Yes."

It had been like this from the beginning.

One touch, one look, and she was done in. This man had brought her happiness she'd never imagined. As she soared higher and higher, almost at the pinnacle, she clasped him to her.

"I love you."

"And I adore you, my beloved wife."

The wave crashed over her, his peak following an instant later.

Once she'd caught her breath, she rested her chin on his chest and ran her fingers through the crisp hair there. "Do you think the legend of the Blue Damask rose is real?"

"How can it not be, my darling? We should have been enemies, but look at us." He brushed his fingertips over the swell of her breasts. "A love like ours is as rare and wonderful as the Blue Damask. It's legendary."

Groggy with contentment, she snuggled into his side. "I like that. A legendary love— forever and always."

About the Author

USA Today Bestselling, award-winning author COLLETTE CAMERON® scribbles Scottish and Regency historicals featuring dashing rogues and scoundrels and the intrepid damsels who re-form them. Blessed with an overactive and witty muse that won't stop whispering new romantic romps in her ear, she's lived in Oregon her entire life, though she dreams of living in Scotland part-time. A self-confessed Cadbury chocoholic, you'll always find a dash of inspiration and a pinch of humor in her sweet-to-spicy timeless romances®.

Explore **Collette's worlds** at
www.collettecameron.com!

Join her **VIP Reader Club** and **FREE newsletter**.
Giggles guaranteed!

FREE BOOK: Join Collette's The Regency Rose®
VIP Reader Club to get updates on book releases,
cover reveals, contests and giveaways she reserves
exclusively for email and newsletter followers. Also,
any deals, sales, or special promotions are offered to
club members first. She will not share your name or
email, nor will she spam you.

http://bit.ly/TheRegencyRoseGift

From the Desk of Collette Cameron

Dearest Reader,

I'm so delighted you've chosen to read Chester and Eden's story, ***A Rose for a Rogue***. I adored Lord Sterling in ***The Rogue and the Wallflower***, and though he didn't win the heroine in that tale, I decided he'd have his own story someday.

As was true of most women during the Regency Era, Eden and her mother had little recourse but to accept the stipend Walter Andrews bestowed upon them. While women today have options available if they find themselves in circumstances similar to what Eden and her mother faced, such was not the case in the early 1800s.

I strive to create stories as historically accurate as possible. Respectable employment was difficult for women to acquire back then, let alone a job that could provide enough income to support a household. That's one reason why London's streets teemed with prostitutes.

While some readers might be offended or frustrated at the lack of choices I offered in this story, my intent was to create believable characters and situations for that time period. To impose today's standards and norms on a prior era, I cannot and will not do.

I hope you enjoyed getting to know Chester and his sweetheart as they struggled to overcome their obstacles to true love.

Please consider telling other readers why you enjoyed this book by reviewing it. Not only do I truly want to hear your thoughts, reviews are crucial for an author to succeed. **Even if you only leave a line or two, I'd very much appreciate it.**

So, with that I'll leave you.

Here's wishing you many happy hours of reading, more happily-ever-afters than you can possibly enjoy in a lifetime, and abundant blessings to you and your loved-ones.

Collette Cameron

A Kiss for a Rogue

The Honorable Rogues®, Book One

Formerly titled A Kiss for Miss Kingsley

**A lonely wallflower. A future viscount.
A second chance at love.**

Olivia Kingsley didn't expect to be swept off her feet and receive a marriage proposal two weeks into her first Season. However, one delicious dance with Allen Wimpleton, and her future is sealed. Or so she thinks until her eccentric father suddenly announces he's moving the family to the Caribbean for a year.

Terrified of losing Olivia, Allen begs her to elope, but she refuses. Distraught at her leaving, and unaware of her father's ill-health, Allen doubts her love and foolishly demands she choose—him or her father.

Heartbroken at his callousness, Olivia turns her back on their love. The year becomes three, enough time for her broken heart to heal, and after her father dies, she returns to England.

Coming face to face with Allen at a ball, she realizes she never purged him from her heart.

But can they overcome their pasts and old wounds to trust love again? Or has Allen found another in her absence?

Excerpt

Enjoy the first chapter of
A Kiss for a Rogue
The Honorable Rogues®, Book One

*A lady must never forget her
manners nor lose her composure.
~A Lady's Guide to Proper Comportment*

1

*London, England
Late May, 1818*

"This is a monumental mistake."

God's toenails. What were you thinking, Olivia Kingsley, agreeing to Auntie Muriel's addlepated scheme?

Why had she ever agreed to this farce?

Fingering the heavy ruby pendant hanging at the hollow of her neck, Olivia peeked out the window as the conveyance rounded the corner onto Berkeley Square. Good God. Carriage upon carriage, like great shiny beetles, lined the street beside an ostentatious manor. Her heart skipped a long beat, and she ducked out of sight.

Braving another glance from the window's corner, her stomach pitched worse than a ship amid a hurricane. The full moon's milky light, along with the mansion's rows of glowing diamond-shaped panes, illuminated the street. Dignified guests in their evening finery swarmed before the grand entrance and on the granite stairs as they waited their turn to enter Viscount and Viscountess Wimpleton's home.

The manor had acquired a new coat of paint since she had seen it last. She didn't care for the pale lead shade, preferring the previous color, a pleasant, welcoming bronze green. Why anyone living in Town would choose to wrap their home in such a chilly color was beyond her. With its enshrouding fog and perpetually overcast skies, London boasted every shade of gray already.

Three years in the tropics, surrounded by vibrant flowers, pristine powdery beaches, a turquoise sea, and balmy temperatures had rather spoiled her against London's grime and stench. How long before she grew accustomed to the dank again? The gloom? The smell?

Never.

Shivering, Olivia pulled her silk wrap snugger. Though late May, she'd been nigh on to freezing since the ship docked last week.

A few curious guests turned to peer in their carriage's direction. A lady swathed in gold silk and dripping diamonds, spoke into her companion's ear and pointed at the gleaming carriage. Did she suspect someone other than Aunt Muriel sat behind the distinctive Daventry crest?

Trepidation dried Olivia's mouth and tightened her chest. Would many of the *ton* remember her?

Stupid question, that. Of course she would be remembered.

Much like ivy—its vines clinging tenaciously to a tree—or a barnacle cemented to a rock, one couldn't easily be pried from the upper ten thousand's memory. But, more on point, would anyone recall her fascination with Allen Wimpleton?

Inevitably.

Coldness didn't cause the new shudder rippling from her shoulder to her waist.

Yes. Attending the ball was a featherbrained solicitation for disaster. No good could come of it. Flattening against the sky-blue and gold-trimmed velvet squab in the corner of her aunt's coach, Olivia vehemently shook her head.

"I cannot do it. I thought I could, but I positively cannot."

A curl came loose, plopping onto her forehead.

Bother.

The dratted, rebellious nuisance that passed for her hair escaped its confines more often than not. She shoved the annoying tendril beneath a pin, having no doubt the tress would work its way free again before evenings end. Patting the circlet of rubies adorning her hair, she assured herself the band remained secure. The treasure had belonged to Aunt Muriel's mother, a

Prussian princess, and no harm must come to it.

Olivia's pulse beat an irregular staccato as she searched for a plausible excuse for refusing to attend the ball after all. She wouldn't lie outright, which ruled out her initial impulse to claim a *megrim*.

"I ... we—" She wiggled her white-gloved fingers at her brother, lounging on the opposite seat. "Were not invited."

Contented as their fat cat, Socrates, after lapping a saucer of fresh cream, Bradford settled his laughing gaze on her. "Yes, we mustn't do anything untoward."

Terribly vulgar, that. Arriving at a *haut ton* function, no invitation in hand. She and Bradford mightn't make it past the vigilant majordomo, and then what were they to do? Scuttle away like unwanted pests? Mortifying and prime tinder for the gossips.

"Whatever will people *think*?" Bradford thrived on upending Society. If permitted, he would dance naked as a robin to see the reactions. He cocked a cinder-black brow, his gray-blue eyes holding a challenge.

Toad.

Olivia yearned to tell him to stop giving her that

loftier look. Instead, she bit her tongue to keep from sticking it out at him like she had as a child. Irrationality warred with reason, until her common sense finally prevailed. "I wouldn't want to impose, is all I meant."

"Nonsense, darling. It's perfectly acceptable for you and Bradford to accompany me." The seat creaked as Aunt Muriel, the Duchess of Daventry, bent forward to scrutinize the crowd. She patted Olivia's knee. "Lady Wimpleton is one of my dearest friends. Why, we had our come-out together, and I'm positive had she known that you and Bradford had recently returned to England, she would have extended an invitation herself."

Olivia pursed her lips.

Not if she knew the volatile way her son and I parted company, she wouldn't have.

A powerful peeress, few risked offending Aunt Muriel, and she knew it well. She could haul a haberdasher or a milkmaid to the ball and everyone would paste artificial smiles on their faces and bid the duo a pleasant welcome. Reversely, if someone earned her scorn, they had best pack-up and leave London permanently before doors began slamming in their faces. Her influence rivaled that of the Almack's patronesses.

Bradford shifted, presenting Olivia with his striking profile as he, too, took in the hubbub before the manor. "You will never be at peace—never be able to move on—unless you do this."

That morsel of knowledge hadn't escaped her, which was why she had agreed to the scheme to begin with. Nevertheless, that didn't make seeing Allen Wimpleton again any less nerve-wracking.

"You must go in, Livy," Bradford urged, his countenance now entirely brotherly concern.

She stopped plucking at her mantle and frowned. "Please don't call me that, Brady."

Once, a lifetime ago, Allen had affectionately called her Livy—until she had refused to succumb to his begging and run away to Scotland. Regret momentarily altered her heart rhythm.

Bradford hunched one of his broad shoulders and scratched his eyebrow. "What harm can come of it?

We'll only stay as long as you like, and I promise, I shall remain by your side the entire time."

Their aunt's unladylike snort echoed throughout the carriage.

"And the moon only shines in the summer." Her voice dry as desert sand, and skepticism peaking her eyebrows high on her forehead, Aunt Muriel fussed with her gloves. "Nephew, I have never known you to forsake an opportunity to become, er . . ."

She slid Olivia a guarded glance. "Shall we say, become better acquainted with the ladies? This Season, there are several tempting beauties and a particularly large assortment of amiable young widows eager for a *distraction*."

Did Aunt Muriel truly believe Olivia don't know about Bradford's reputation with females? She was neither blind nor ignorant.

He turned and flashed their aunt one of his dazzling smiles, his deeply tanned face making it all the more brighter. "All pale in comparison to you two lovelies, no doubt."

Olivia made an impolite noise and, shaking her

head, aimed her eyes heavenward in disbelief.

Doing it much too brown. Again.

Bradford was too charming by far—one reason the fairer sex were drawn to him like ants to molasses. She'd been as doe-eyed and vulnerable when it came to Allen.

"Tish tosh, young scamp. Your compliments are wasted on me." Still, Aunt Muriel slanted her head, a pleased smile hovered on her lightly-painted mouth and pleating the corners of her eyes. "Besides, if you attach yourself to your sister, she won't have an opportunity to find herself alone with young Wimpleton."

Olivia managed to keep her jaw from unhinging as she gaped at her aunt. She snapped her slack mouth shut with an audible click. "Shouldn't you be cautioning me *not* to be alone with a gentleman?"

Aunt Muriel chuckled and patted Olivia's knee again. "That rather defeats the purpose in coming tonight then, doesn't it, dear?" Giving a naughty wink, she nudged Olivia. "I do hope Wimpleton kisses you. He's such a handsome young man. Quite the

Corinthian too."

A hearty guffaw escaped Bradford, and he slapped his knee. "Aunt Muriel, I refuse to marry until I find a female as colorful as you. Life would never be dull."

"I should say not. Daventry and I had quite the adventurous life. It's in my blood, you know, and yours too, I suspect. Papa rode his stallion right into a church and actually snatched Mama onto his lap moments before she was forced to marry an abusive lecher. The scandal, they say, was utterly delicious." The duchess sniffed, a put-upon expression on her lined face. "Dull indeed. *Hmph*. Never. Why, I may have to be vexed with you the entire evening for even hinting such a preposterous thing."

"Grandpapa abducted Grandmamma? In church, no less?" Bradford dissolved into another round of hearty laughter, something he did often as evidenced by the lines near his eyes.

Unable to utter a single sensible rebuttal, Olivia swung her gaze between them. Her aunt and brother beamed, rather like two naughty imps, not at all abashed at having been caught with their mouth's full of stolen sweetmeats from the kitchen.

She wrinkled her nose and gave a dismissive flick of her wrist. "Bah. You two are completely hopeless where decorum is concerned."

"Don't mistake decorum for stodginess or pomposity, my dear." Her aunt gave a sage nod. "Neither permits a mite of fun and both make one a cantankerous boor."

Bradford snickered again, his hair, slightly too long for London, brushing his collar. "By God, if only there were more women like you."

Olivia itched to box his ears. Did he take nothing seriously?

No. Not since Philomena had died.

Olivia edged near the window once more and worried the flesh of her lower lip. Carriages continued to line up, two or three abreast. Had the entire *beau monde* turned out for the grand affair?

Botheration. Why must the Wimpletons be so well-received?

She caught site of her tense face reflected in the glass, and hastily turned away.

"And, Aunt Muriel, you're absolutely positive that Allen—that is, Mr. Wimpleton—remains unattached?"

Fiddling with her shawl's silk fringes, Olivia attempted a calming breath. No force on heaven or earth could compel her to enter the manor if Allen were betrothed or married to another. Her fragile heart, though finally mended after three years of painful healing, could bear no more anguish or regret.

If he were pledged to another, she would simply take the carriage back to Aunt Muriel's, pack her belongings, and make for Bromham Hall, Bradford's newly inherited country estate. Olivia would make a fine spinster; perhaps even take on the task of housekeeper in order to be of some use to her brother. She would never set foot in Town again.

She dashed her aunt an impatient, sidelong peek. Why didn't Aunt Muriel answer the question?

Head to the side and eyes brimming with compassion, Aunt Muriel regarded her.

"You're certain he's not courting anyone?" Olivia pressed for the truth. "There's no one he has paid marked attention to? You must tell me, mustn't fear for my sensibilities or that I'll make a scene."

She didn't make scenes.

The *A Lady's Guide to Proper Comportment* was most emphatic in that regard.

Only the most vulgar and lowly bred indulge in histrionics or emotional displays.

Aunt Muriel shook her turbaned head firmly. The bold ostrich feather topping the hair covering jolted violently, and her diamond and emerald cushion-shaped earrings swung with the force of her movement. She adjusted her gaudily-colored shawl.

"No. No one. Not from the lack of enthusiastic mamas, and an audacious papa or two, shoving their simpering daughters beneath his nose, I can tell you. Wimpleton's considered a brilliant catch, quite dashing, and a top-sawyer, to boot." She winked wickedly again. "Why, if I were only a score of years younger ..."

"Yes? What *would* you do, Aunt Muriel?" Rubbing his jaw, Bradford grinned.

Olivia flung him a flinty-eyed glare. "Hush. Do not encourage her."

Worse than children, the two of them.

Lips pursed, Aunt Muriel ceased fussing with her skewed pendant and tapped her fingers upon her plump thigh. "I would wager a year's worth of my favorite pastries that fast Rossington chit has set her cap for him, though. Has her feline claws dug in deep, too, I fear."

A Bride for a Rogue

The Honorable Rogues®, Book Two

Formerly titled Bride of Falcon

She can't forget the past. He can't face the future. Until fate intervenes one night.

Many years ago, Ivonne Wimpleton loved Chancy Faulkenhurst and hoped to marry him. Then one day, without any explanation, he sailed to India. Now, after five unsuccessful Seasons and a riding accident that left her with a slight limp, her only suitors are fortune-hunters and degenerates. Just as Ivy's resigned herself to spinsterhood, Chance unexpectedly returns.

Upon returning to England, Chance is disillusioned, disfigured, and emotionally scarred, but his love for Ivy remains is strong. However, he's failed to acquire the fortune he sought in order to earn permission to marry her. When he discovers Ivy's being forced to wed to prevent a scandalous secret from being revealed, he's determined to make her his bride.

Except, believing Chance made no effort to contact her all those years, Ivy's furious with him. What's more, in his absence, his father arranged a profitable marriage for Chance. As he battles his own inner demons, he must convince Ivy to risk loving him again. But will their parents' interference jeopardize Chance and Ivy's happiness once more?

A Rogue's Scandalous Wish
The Honorable Rogues®, Book Three

Formerly titled Her Scandalous Wish

**A marriage offered out of obligation…
…an acceptance compelled by desperation.**

At the urging of her dying brother, Philomena Pomfrett reluctantly agrees to attend a London Season. If she fails to acquire a husband, her future is perilous. Betrayed once by Bradford, Viscount Kingsley, as well as scarred from a horrific fire, Philomena entertains no notions of a love-match. Hers will be a marriage of convenience. *If* she can find man who will have her.

When the woman he loves dies, Bradford leaves England and its painful memories behind. After a three-year absence, he returns home but doesn't recognize his first love when he stumbles upon her hiding in a shadowy arbor during a ball. Something about the mysterious woman enthralls him, and he steals a moonlit kiss. Caught in the act by Philomena's brother, Bradford is issued an ultimatum—a duel or marry her.

Bradford refuses to duel with a gravely-ill man and offers marriage. But Philomena rejects his half-hearted proposal, convinced he'd grow to despise her when he sees her disfiguring scars. Then her brother collapses, and frantic to provide the medical care he needs, she's faced with marrying a man who deserted her once already.

To Capture a Rogue's Heart

The Honorable Rogues®, Book Four

Formerly titled To Tame a Scoundrel's Heart

**He recruited her to help him find a wife...
...and discovered she was the perfect candidate.**

Her betrothed cheated on her.
Katrina Needham intended to marry her beloved major and live happily-ever-after—until he's seen with another woman. Distraught, and needing a distraction, she agrees to assist the rugged, and dangerously handsome Captain Dominic St. Monté find a wife. So why does she find herself entertaining romantic notions about the privateer turned duke?

He believed he was illegitimate.
When Nic unexpectedly inherits a dukedom and the care of his young sisters, he reluctantly decides he must marry. Afterward, if his new duchess is willing, he hopes to return to the sea-faring life he craves part-time. If she doesn't agree, he'll have no choice but to give up the sea forever.

Will they forsake everything for each other?
Nic soon realizes Katrina possesses every characteristic he seeks in a duchess. The more time he spends with the vivacious beauty, the more enamored he becomes. Still, he cannot ask for her hand. Not only is she still officially promised to another, she has absolutely no interest in becoming a duchess, much less a privateer's wife.

Can Nic and Katrina relinquish their carefully planned futures and trust love to guide them?

The Rogue and the Wallflower

The Honorable Rogues®, Book Five

Formerly titled The Wallflower's Wicked Wager

He loved her beyond anything and everything—precisely why he must never marry her.

Love—sentimental drivel for weak, feckless fools.
Since an explosion ravaged Captain Morgan Le Draco's face and cost him his commission in the Royal Dragoons, he's fortified himself behind a rampart of cynicism and distrust. He's put aside all thoughts of marrying until he risks his life to save a drowning woman. At once, Morgan knows Shona's the balm for his tortured soul. But as a wealthy noblewoman, she's far above his humble station and can never be his.

Love—a treasured gift reserved for those beautiful of form and face.
Scorned and ridiculed most of her adult life, Shona Atterberry believes she's utterly undesirable and is reconciled to spinsterhood. She hides her spirited

temperament beneath a veneer of shyness. Despite how ill-suited they are, and innuendos that Captain Le Draco is a fortune-hunter, she cannot escape her growing fascination.

Two damaged souls searching for love.
Shona is goaded into placing a wicked wager. One that sets her upon a ruinous path and alienates the only man who might have ever loved her. Is true love enough to put their pasts behind them, to learn to trust, and to heal their wounded hearts.

Printed in Great Britain
by Amazon